Birthday Pie

A Novel

ARTHUR WOOTEN

GALAXIAS PRODUCTIONS

Birthday Pie
A Novel

Galaxias Productions
200 West 90ᵗʰ Street Suite 9B
New York, NY 10024

ISBN: 978-0-9835631-4-3

Graphic Art by: Bud Santora

For Gert

The Martindales
of
Ragland

King-Battles-Martindale Family Tree

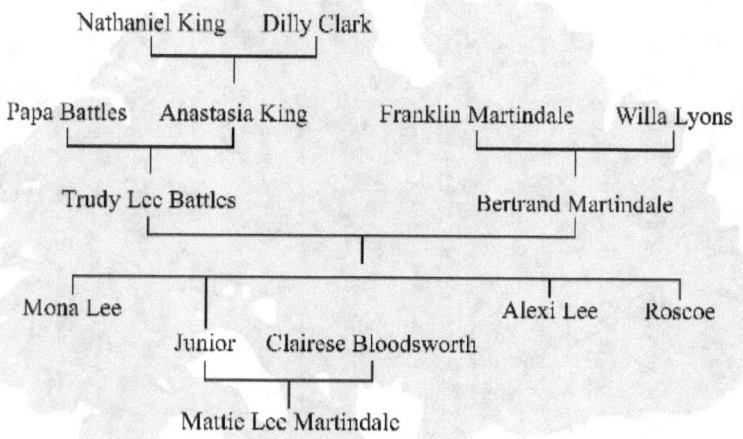

CONTENTS

ONE

MEET THE MARTINDALES

Her claim to fame was that she was fourth runner-up Miss North
Carolina 1944. And now, at age sixty-four, Trudy Lee Martindale
was still acting the part. With her hair wrapped in a pink towel, a
tiara perched on top of that, and a mudpack on her face, she
slipped her left foot out of the luxurious bubble bath and turned
on the hot water with her big toe.

*"I believe in doing what I can, in crying when I must, in laughing
when I choose. Heigh-ho, if love were all, I should be lonely..."*

That was her song. Noel Coward's *If Love Were All*. And she
thought it summed up her life. Never in her wildest nightmares
did she ever think that in 1990 she would still be living in Ragland, the town she grew up in, right smack dab in the middle of
tobacco country. She took another sip of bourbon and glanced
over at her vanity.

There were atomizers full of cloyingly sweet perfumes, bottles
of make-up and jars of cold cream. Mascaras, rouges, powder puffs
and brushes. False eyelashes, colored pencils, concealers and
shadows. And at least a dozen tubes of lipstick, all in the same
color. Shimmering Pink. And wedged in between the blonde wig-

let and the Aqua Net was a picture of Trudy Lee and Lex smiling a little too hard. Taken fifteen years earlier you could see how much he resembled his mother.

"Thank God you inherited my small facial features, darling. You'll stay young-looking forever," she declared as she lifted her glass to the picture. "Hurry home, Alexi Lee. It's time to celebrate."

*   *   *   *

Up in his New York City apartment, he was throwing clothes into a suitcase in a panic to get to the airport. Although the smallest of the Martindale men, standing only five-feet-eight inches tall, Lex was always delighted when people thought he was taller. Few knew he stood so erect because a steel rod had been drilled into his spine after a gymnastics injury when he was seventeen.

With his light brown hair sheared short and dressed all in black, he was going home on the last of the many trips that he sarcastically had dubbed "the death runs."

"I know I'm forgetting something." Lex ran his hand over his scalp and then looked at his palm. "Great, another clump of hair."

"Laxatives?" suggested his lover Peter.

"Right. I always need help when I go back to Ragland."

Peter smiled. "I'll get them for you."

They had just celebrated their fifth anniversary. Although neither of them was still in love with the other and both were mimicking their parents' dysfunctional relationships, they did love one another. And in a time of uncertainty, they held onto each other tightly for comfort and security.

Peter returned with the laxatives as the house phone in the kitchen buzzed.

"Peter, can you get that?"

He ran down the hallway, through the dining room and into the eat-in kitchen. They lived on the top floor-through apartment of an historic brownstone located on Perry Street in Greenwich Village. Although it was in desperate need of a complete gut job, and all work had been put on hold due to long-delayed work permits, Lex found the chaos and disarray disturbingly familiar.

"Yes?" Peter asked while pressing the intercom.

"Car service."

"He'll be right down."

Lex dropped his suitcase in the front hall.

"Is he early or am I late?"

"Both," Peter laughed. "Now calm down."

"Do I have everything?"

"What about your drugs?"

"My God I forgot. Lets see, ten days, forty pills..." Lex started running in place. "Ooooh, damn it. I knew this would happen. I've got to pee again. Will you get them for me?"

Lex ran off to the bathroom as Peter opened a kitchen cupboard displaying a plethora of medications, and took out several bottles of pills.

* * * *

Meanwhile, back in Ragland and out of her bath, Trudy Lee sat at her vanity applying a heavy layer of foundation to her face. She had slipped into a pink chenille bathrobe, a pair of pink mule pumps, and had her blonde hair up in curlers while she continued to sing her song.

"I believe, the more you love a man, the more you give your trust, the more you're bound to lose..."

She took a sip of her bourbon and whispered through her teeth, "Well, ain't that the God's honest truth?"

* * * *

Looking at his watch, Lex raced out of his building followed by

Peter, and threw his bag into the cab.

"Lex, you sure you don't want me to come?"

"I wouldn't do that to you," he laughed.

Lex jumped into the car and rolled down the window.

"Then we'll celebrate your birthday when you get back?"

"It's a date," smiled Lex.

"You're going to tell your mother, aren't you?"

Lex gave him a stern look. "Yes."

"Well, don't get mad. She has a right to know."

"You've asked me ten times and I've answered you ten times. Yes, I'm going to tell Trudy Lee."

The driver knocked on the partition. "Which airport?"

"La Guardia, please. "

The car sped off. Looking back through the rear window at Peter, Lex's smile faded, making him look more like a frightened child than a man of thirty-six years.

* * * *

Earlier that morning out in Los Angeles, Lex's older sister, Mona Lee, was having her own troubles getting home to Ragland.

"What is the problem?" she screamed at the cabby.

The driver sat taller and then adjusted his rear view mirror trying to see the person barking orders from the back seat. All that was visible was the top of her head.

A new-age junkie, Mona Lee stood four-feet-eight inches tall and was partial to silks and satins in bright oranges and reds. Thin and sinewy from years of being macro-neurotic, she had a rather pinched look to her face. With black hair and fluorescent-green eyes she appeared more Mediterranean than Anglo-Saxon. In fact, considering how she was dressed now, she could have easily been mistaken for a Spanish gypsy, except for the purple turban on her head.

"I'm sorry, lady, but we're stuck in traffic," he explained to, what to him, looked like a floating bowling ball.

"Well, if you had taken the route I asked you to, none of this would have happened." She struggled to pull herself up to the clear plastic divider. "And I am not a lady!" She fell back against the seat.

"You can say that again."

The purple bowling ball perked up. "What was that?"

"Nothing," grumbled the cabby.

"I am a *woman*." She rolled down her window and stuck her head out.

Suddenly, a police car came barreling along the shoulder of the highway with its siren screaming.

"Jesus Christ!" she screamed as she sank back down into the seat. Beads of sweat trickled down her face as she started to tremble.

"You OK...woman?" asked the cabby.

Mona Lee was desperate. Desperate to get out of Los Angeles. For two reasons. One, just having graduated from the Pacific Rim Shiatsu Institute, she wanted to rush home and cure her daddy of cancer. Two, just having graduated from the Pacific Rim Shiatsu Institute, she'd been working on a new client the day before and had heard that he had passed away shortly after her session. Mona Lee was on the lam.

She peeked out of the window again. The police having vanished, she breathed a sigh of relief.

"That was close." However, the traffic had come to a dead halt. "Driver? I want you to creatively visualize clear highways from here to LAX."

"You what?"

"Just shut your eyes and use mind control."

Dumbfounded, he stared at her in the rear view mirror.

"I said shut your eyes!"

He closed his eyes, as did Mona Lee.

"Now I want you to picture a blank screen in front of you."

"A what?"

"Like a movie screen but blank. And on that screen I want you to project the image of a clear highway. Can you do that?"

"I'll try."

"Now, see our cab moving along this empty stretch of highway. Do you see it?"

"Yes. Yes, I see it."

The cab inched forward very slowly.

She whispered, "Good. Now, picture us traveling at a speed...," suddenly she screamed at the top of her lungs, "...that will get me to the airport so I don't miss this freaking plane!"

And with that, the driver with his eyes still closed, floored the cab and they crashed into the car in front of them.

* * * *

Back in Ragland, Trudy Lee emerged from a pile of hatboxes that had come crashing down onto her in the walk-in closet. There were rows and rows of every style and color of shoe imaginable as well as racks upon racks crammed with everything from formal gowns to satin negligees.

Wearing a Victoria's Secret push-up bra, panties and with her hair still in curlers, Trudy Lee struggled to her feet. She grabbed a pressed pair of designer denim jeans and a powder-pink button-down blouse and tripped over a pair of knee-high boots, coming out of the closet.

She dropped the jeans onto the floor and stepped into each pant leg. She shimmied them up to her hips and then lay flat on the bed. She squiggled and squirmed and with the strength of ten men, pulled the jeans up over her butt. Sucking in her stomach she zipped up the fly. Unable to either button them or sit up, she rolled onto her stomach, slid off the bed, hopped over to her dresser and secured the waist with a large safety pin.

"God damn dryer cooks everything till it's two sizes too

small."

* * * *

At this same moment, Trudy Lee's mother, Anastasia Battles, was on a flight down to North Carolina from Michigan. A widow for almost two decades, she had moved to Detroit to be close to her three-out-of-ten siblings that were still alive. Vegetables in nursing homes, but still alive. Anastasia's friends in her hometown of Winston-Salem, still shook their heads and spat in the dirt when they thought of her crossing the line and moving up into Yankee territory.

At eighty-five, she was nearly blind from macular degeneration. With Coke-bottle-thick eyeglasses and with the kindness of strangers, she still was able to live alone in a one-bedroom apartment.

Wearing a bright red suit and matching hat and with a huge, red plastic patent leather purse hanging on her forearm, she downed another gin and tonic.

"Don't you just love drinking alcohol on airplanes?" she asked the businessman sitting in the aisle seat next to her.

He nodded politely.

"It makes the buzz that much stronger," she continued. "Speaking of which, I have to use the little girls' room. Would you excuse me?"

The man unbuckled his seat belt and stood up, allowing Anastasia to pass by.

"And could you be a dear and point me in the right direction?"

"It's all the way in the back of the plane, Ma'am."

"Thank you ever so much," she replied as she headed to the front.

"Ma'am?" he shouted.

She stopped and turned around. "Yes?"

"I said the back of the plane."

"Oh, yes. Thank you."

Anastasia teetered towards the back of the plane, hitting passengers in the head with her handbag as she felt for each row of seats.

She passed the galley and the lavatory. Having reached the very back of the plane, she felt the wall and found a door, the emergency exit for the plane.

She knocked on it and called out, "Hello? Hello? Is someone using the bathroom?" She listened hard and then found the release lever that opens the exit and declared, "Speak now or forever hold your piece."

A flight attendant appeared screaming, "Ma'am! Don't touch that door!"

Paying no heed, Anastasia laughed and continued to pull at the lever. Like a seasoned linebacker, the flight attendant tackled Anastasia to the floor as the plane flew over the Indian Ridge, North Carolina Country Club.

* * * *

Down on the course, in a sand trap on the third hole, Roscoe Martindale studied his golf ball with pained seriousness. Trying to make it in the pro-golf world was not coming easily to Trudy Lee's youngest son.

Roscoe would have preferred to be playing on a course in Ragland. That is, if they'd had one. With a scrawny population of just under three thousand four hundred people, and the average family income much less than the national average, Ragland was lucky to have a 7-Eleven, never mind a country club with an Olympic size swimming pool, five-star restaurant and eighteen-hole golf course.

But Indian Ridge was inclusive to few and restrictive to many. So the only way Roscoe could practice on this golf course built on the edge of Ragland was to become a caddy, a job he was embarrassed to have, and which he kept hidden from his family.

A tournament was coming up the following weekend, opening the window for amateurs to advance to professional status, and Roscoe was determined to be one of the lucky few.

Looking pale and thin and playing by himself, he took a practice swing and then pondered the trajectory his ball needed to travel. The distance to the third hole was not far, just tricky. He moved up to the ball, concentrated, looked off towards the hole and then back at the ball. He swung and completely missed it. Self-conscious, he looked to see if anyone had noticed. He stepped up to the ball, concentrated, took another swing and missed the ball again. Flustered, Roscoe swung violently at the ball and missed a third time.

"God damn it!" he cursed. Furious, he threw the club down and kicked the golf ball. It soared through the air as Roscoe hopped up and down holding his foot.

The ball descended, landed on the green and rolled into the hole. Roscoe looked stunned for a moment and then screamed, "Yes!" He continued to rub his foot while looking around to see if anyone was watching.

* * * *

Built in the mid 1700s, the Martindales' two-story, white structure had a wrap-around veranda supported by wide columns. It was a large house with fireplaces in all of the main rooms. Surprising to most people who have never lived in North Carolina, its damp and cold winters can be quite unforgiving. The property sat on several acres of overgrown landscaping bordered with magnolia, pine, beech and oak trees.

Upon entering the front of the house, one was assaulted by the sight of an oversized double staircase leading to the four bedrooms upstairs. To the right was a formal salon. To the left, the dining room. In the back of the house was a large country kitchen sorely aching for a renovation. Off the kitchen was the keeping room, which now functioned as the Martindales' family room. Next to that was a small maid's room with a bath down the hall. And there was an outdoor entrance to the kitchen via the screened back porch.

Although the architect's original intentions were commendable, there was something off about the proportions of the building and the quality of the materials. If Scarlett O'Hara had lived in Tara, then Trudy Lee Martindale now lived in Terror. There was always something breaking down, falling apart and needing repairs.

With her hair combed out into a sixties flip, Trudy Lee descended the back staircase, clutching an assortment of framed photos to her chest. She carefully straddled the fourth from the bottom step and continued down through the kitchen and into the large keeping room. She scurried over to the loveseat and gently placed the pictures down, then dashed to the giant walk-in fireplace that flanked the back wall. Like lightning, she cleared the mantel of all existing photos of family members, then meticulously and lovingly positioned each framed picture that she had brought downstairs into the absolutely perfect position. She stood back and admired the new gallery. They were all photos of Lex.

Trudy Lee glanced over at the grandfather clock that was listing in the far corner of the room and then dashed into the kitchen. Earlier in the day, she had been preparing a pecan pie, when she abandoned the project for her bubble bath. She opened a bottom kitchen cabinet and struggled to push open the drawer that was above it. She pulled out a mallet and moved over to a pile of unshelled pecans, a cooked pie shell, an open bottle of bourbon and a bowl full of wet ingredients. She slipped on an apron and plaintively continued with *If Love Were All*, while smashing the pecans with intense hostility.

"*Although, when shadows fall, I think if only...*" Whack! "*Somebody splendid really needed me...*" Whack! "*Someone affectionate and*

10

dear..." Whack! "*Cares would be ended if I knew that he, wanted to have me near.*" With the last whack, she managed to hit her thumb. "Jesus..."

* * * *

"...fucking Christ!" is what ten-year-old Mattie Lee Martindale blurted out in the middle of her piano recital.

Moments earlier her mother Clairese and father Junior, Trudy Lee's oldest son, were watching proudly as their Mattie Lee, wearing her crushed-velvet, hunter-green jumper and black patent leather shoes, sailed through Chopin's *Prelude No. 26* without a hitch.

Clairese Bloodsworth Martindale was extremely frustrated that at the age of thirty-six she had borne only one child after fifteen years of marriage. Therefore, she poured all of that energy into being Ragland's most perfect domestic engineer. Unfortunately, she should have paid a little more attention to what she was eating. Being five-feet-four inches tall and tipping the scale at close to two hundred and fifty pounds, she filled up the empty corners of her existence with high-calorie processed food and had never exercised a day in her life. And to top that off, she had what she called a deviated septum, causing her voice to always sound nasal.

She also had the very annoying habit of dressing just like her daughter. Today she had the cute pixie haircut and the black patent Mary Janes, but her hunter-green jumper looked more like an oversized sofa slipcover than a chic dress.

She was a simple yet complicated woman born to a family of overachievers. Her father was a professor of American History, her mother a successful cookbook author. Her brothers became doctors, her sister a lawyer. In college, Clairese took a stab at the medical profession. She struggled through pre-med and then decided to specialize in ophthalmology. But very late in the game she discovered that she had no eye for it. So she quit graduate school and tried her hand at interior decorating. Unfortunately, she had no eye for that either.

However, at an early age, she did realize that she had one very strong attribute: the ability to wrap anyone around her little finger. If she had been brighter she could have been a brilliant politician. Or, at the very least, a crooked one. But instead, she chose to be the world's most perfectly horrifying wife and mother.

A native of Ragland, she and Junior had known each other since nursery school. Back then, when she had slipped her construction paper wedding ring around Junior's pudgy little finger and stated, "You'll marry me," she wasn't kidding. Junior didn't have a fighting chance. Until now.

But halfway through this very difficult piece, their child prodigy began to falter. Clairese grabbed the cuff of Junior's smallish business suit, which befitted this overweight certified public accountant, and dug her nails into his flesh.

To her mother's horror, Mattie Lee stopped playing altogether. She glanced out into the audience with what looked like a smirk, then tried to pick up where she had left off. After a few notes she stopped again.

As the audience sat in embarrassed and complete silence, no one had a bit of trouble hearing Mattie Lee blurt out her second rendition of, "Jesus fucking…"

* * * *

"…Christ that hurt," Trudy Lee exclaimed while sucking her thumb. She took down a glass from the cupboard and poured herself another bourbon.

Just then her kitchen phone rang. She took a quick sip, let it ring once more and then answered it in her best Marilyn Monroe voice.

"Happy Birthday, Alexi Lee Martindale."

Lex had just landed at Raleigh/Durham International Airport and couldn't figure out why there were hordes of people swarming everywhere. He covered his other ear, trying to hear her better. "Mother, now how did you know it was me?"

"I recognized your ring." Suddenly her tone sounded a bit anxious. "You are still coming, aren't you?"

"Of course I am." A man in a motorized wheelchair grazed Lex's leg. "Hey watch it! In fact, I'm here. At the airport right now."

Looking at the kitchen clock, Trudy Lee hurriedly threw the shelled pecans into the mixing bowl and stirred aggressively.

"You're here already? But I thought your flight got in at 6:20?"

She measured two tablespoons of bourbon and splashed them into the bowl. She hesitated, then poured bourbon straight from the bottle into the mixture.

"Well, I was supposed to." A woman traveling alone with five children stopped in front of Lex as her youngest began to wail. "I got to La Guardia two hours before my flight, thanks to Peter's obsessive-compulsive neurotic fear that no one can get to the airport too soon, and I jumped onto an earlier flight."

"Gee, Lex, this throws a monkey wrench into everything."

"Look, if my being here is a problem, I can go back to New York," he threatened with an edge to his voice. He made an evil face at the crying brat standing before him, which sent the kid running down the terminal.

"Now don't get testy, Lex. Of course it's all right. Oh, but darling, I look awful. I've lost weight but I'm so fat. You'll hate the way I look." She poured bourbon into her highball glass and took a swallow.

"I'm sure you look fine. How's Dad?"

"I think he's sleeping, the poor guy." She looked over at the half-closed door to the maid's room.

Trudy Lee's voice pierced through his emaciated body as his

gnarled fingers struggled to untie the drawstring of his pajama bottoms. With great difficulty, he reached into his pajamas and painfully pulled out a catheter. He moaned and gasped for breath. Having been diagnosed with advanced lung cancer, which had quickly spread to the rest of his vital organs, Bert Martindale had opted for no further treatment and to die at home.

Once a strong and muscular athlete, he now looked like a walking bag of bones. Within the last year most of his beautiful salt-and-pepper hair had fallen out, his muscles had atrophied and his strong, chiseled looks had disappeared. It was as if the cancer had come along and was erasing him.

With nothing more than a hospital bed, nightstand, one light and a dresser, he was living out the rest of his days in this dark and Spartan room. His one request had been to have a giant map of the world tacked up onto the wall facing the bed. The family assumed that his desire to stay in the maid's room was to eliminate the need to go up and down stairs, which was partly true. But what he also wanted, hoped for, was peace and solitude.

Trudy Lee's whisper resonated throughout his room. "I just want to warn you Lex, the doctor said it's going to be any moment now and it's not pretty."

Fuck you, Bert screamed at her inside his head. He swung his legs over the side of the bed and struggled to get to his feet. He leaned forward, trying to gather enough strength to push away from the mattress.

"And the Midge is coming in from L.A.," Trudy Lee informed Lex as she poured the mixture into the pie shell.

"Mother, please don't call her that."

"I'm sorry. Your sister Mona Lee is coming in from L.A."

"Is Roscoe home? Can he pick me up at the airport?"

Roscoe entered from the back porch carrying his bag of beat-up golf clubs. Exhausted, he looked around the room, and seeing that he and Trudy Lee were alone, he smiled at her.

"They revoked his license this time."

14

Roscoe's mood changed instantly. "Do ya gotta tell the whole fucking world?"

"It's not the whole world." She waved him over. "It's my Lex. Come say hello to him."

"Why?"

She held the receiver out to him as he threw the clubs down onto the floor and ran up the staircase, hopping over the fourth step.

Lex rolled his eyes, easily picturing the scenario unfolding. "Mother, can you come get me?"

"Lex, my car's in the shop."

"What about Junior?"

"He and Clairese are at Mattie Lee's piano recital. You'll have to take a cab."

"Is Vladimir still the only...?"

"What do you have against Vladimir?"

Lex dropped his forehead into his hand. "I have nothing against Vladimir, Mother. It's just that he won't bring me up the drive to the house."

She poured a dash of bourbon into the bowl, paused and then poured more. "Russians work almost as hard as the rest of us. There's no need to be prejudiced, Lex."

He shook his head. "I'm not the prejudiced..."

"In fact, he's quite the renaissance man."

"Huh?"

Trudy Lee took her Shimmering Pink lipstick out of her apron pocket and applied a layer. "Hurry, Lex. I can't wait to see you."

"I love you?" he said questioningly.

"Me too, you." Trudy Lee giggled as she kissed twice and hung up the phone.

Lex slowly put the receiver down, leaned his forehead against the payphone and closed his eyes. He took a deep breath, opened them, and noticed the men's room across the terminal. He picked up his bag and walked towards it.

While humming *If Love Were All,* Trudy Lee joyfully poured herself a glass of the bourbon and took a swallow. She gave the wet ingredients a big stir and poured them into the pie shell. Pie in hand, she bent over and opened the oven, when suddenly there was a violent crash against the maid's room door, causing it to slam shut. Startled, she dropped the pie and it spilled onto the floor.

"Oh shit," she whispered.

There was a weak banging against the door. Trudy Lee started towards the bedroom then looked back at the pie mixture on the linoleum floor. She ran back to it and thought for a moment.

When's the last time I washed this floor?

Shaking her head, she quickly knelt down, scooped the sticky mess into her hands, scraped it into the pie pan, and threw all of it into the oven.

The banging from the maid's room got louder.

"I'm coming, for Christ's sake."

Opting not to clean up the remaining uncooked pie on the floor, she took another swallow of bourbon as the noise got louder.

"Will you please stop that banging, Bert?"

The doorknob started to turn as Trudy Lee reached for it.

"I'm here. I'm here."

She opened the door and Bert was down on all fours. He attempted to crawl out of the room.

"Golly Bert, you can't keep getting out of bed. Where do you think you're going?"

He looked up at her pathetically.

"You pulled that tube out again?" He nodded. "Then why won't you use the bedpan?"

She bent down and grabbed Bert under his arms and helped him to his feet. Step by painful step, Trudy Lee supported him with her outstretched arms as she walked him backwards down the hall to the bathroom. Although he couldn't have weighed more than seventy-five pounds, it took all of her strength to hold him up.

"That's it. One step at a time. Do you want your cigarettes and beer?"

He nodded yes.

"Slow down, Bert. Take it easy. Do you know who that was on the phone?"

He shook his head.

"Lex. Today's his birthday. Not that you'd care. You never did. I think he's twenty-nine. No, twenty-eight. Did I tell you his book is doing great? They think it will reach the bestseller list by next week. I'm so disappointed his friend Peter isn't coming. He looks so handsome in his pictures. Their apartment is supposed to be gorgeous. You know they've invited me up, but you with your condition, well I certainly can't leave now, can I? The Midge is coming in on a later flight. And my Mother Superior is flying down from Detroit. Oh God, I don't know how I'll handle the two of them at the same time, judging and criticizing my every move. I'll just keep breathing. That's what my Lex says to do. He says it's essential to life. To keep breathing. Just like this."

She took a deep breath, which triggered off a coughing attack.

"Damn you, Bertrand Martindale. It's your cigarettes that's ruining my health. All that residual smoke. I swear if you give me your lung cancer, I'll kill you!"

Still coughing, she began to lose her strength.

"Oh God, Bert. I don't think we're going to make it."

They both fell to the floor, Bert landing on top of Trudy Lee. There was a moment of silence and then she burst into laughter.

"Oh Bert, we haven't done this in twenty-five years."

He gasped for breath. *Thirty.*

Trudy Lee hollered for help. "Roscoe? Roscoe! Help. Help me!" She screamed louder. "Roscoe!"

Roscoe ran down the stairs and looked at his parents on the

floor. "Nasty. Just nasty."

Trudy Lee tried to catch her breath. "I resent that, Roscoe. I am still very sexual and desirable."

He just stared at them.

"Oh for God's sake, we fell. Now get him off of me."

Roscoe rolled Bert off Trudy Lee. "Hey Pop."

"That's it. Pretend I'm not even here," she exclaimed. "I want to talk to you, young man. The bank called again."

"I played the best game of golf today. A hole in one! Can you beat that, Pop?"

"Roscoe? Did you hear me?" she asked while sitting up. "You can't keep writing checks. You don't have a checking account."

Roscoe gathered Bert into his arms and carried him like a child towards the bathroom.

Still sitting on the floor, Trudy Lee brushed herself off and then looked at her hands. "Oh my God."

"If I keep up like this Pop, I could make easily a million my first year on the pro-circuit," Roscoe said as they disappeared into the bathroom.

"All over me. He peed all over me!" Trudy Lee managed to get up without using her hands, as Roscoe came out of the bathroom and went into the kitchen. "And on Lex's birthday. Now I'll have to change," she cried as she ran up the stairs, skipping the fourth step, with her arms flailing at her sides.

Roscoe came out of the kitchen with a can of beer and a pack of cigarettes. "You'll never change, Mother," he whispered to himself as he went back into the bathroom with Bert.

TWO

THE POLIO PIT

Lex looked at his watch and was surprised at how long he had been sitting in the airport bathroom stall with no results.

Just then, a man entered and stood at the urinal next to his stall. Lex happened to notice that the man was wearing scuffed beige boots. But as time went by, he heard no stream of pee. Fascinated, he could see the man's shadow on the tile floor, cast by the overhead light. From all indications it was clear that he was going to relieve himself of something else.

Lex's heart raced as he decided to join in. Public toilets were not his cup of tea; being a voyeur was. Even as a child he was fascinated with watching people.

At an early age he'd discovered his ability to sneak around Ragland late at night, quiet as a cat burglar. Whether it was watching Chet Brownley cheating on his wife with Barbra Anne Nutt, or witnessing the conception of Buzz and Joyce Pendleton's third child, Paula, or joining in with Corky Nault from the outside of his bedroom window as he played freely and joyfully with himself when his boorish wife Sarah Sue left town to visit her mother, Lex had become unofficially Ragland's little Peeping Tom.

And this addiction carried over into his adult life. Not involving his lover Peter, of course. To him, two was company. No, Lex's voyeurism was his own private obsession. And with one strict rule, only he could watch and no one could know he was watching. And now that he was a confirmed gay man, the "watchee" had to be male.

Careful not to make a sound, Lex held his breath as he watched his partner's shadow and followed his rhythm. But before he knew it, his neighbor gasped and moaned and was out the door as quickly as he had come...in. Deflated in more ways than one, Lex went back to just sitting and waiting for nature to take its course.

Fifteen minutes had passed, and with no results or visitors, Lex pulled up his pants and decided to phone Vladimir, the only cab driver that would make the forty-minute drive due west to Ragland knowing that he'd forfeit a fare on the way back. Vladimir couldn't pass up a dollar.

Vladimir Czarlinsky was an exceptional pole-vaulter representing the USSR during the Olympic Games held in Montreal, Canada in 1976.

Living just outside Moscow, Vladimir had been an accountant. But jobs were scarce, and good paying jobs were nonexistent. Drawing in a measly income that, in US currency, translated into approximately $5.20 a month, he was forced, as were many other lower-middle-class Russians, to live with his family. His entire family. Which meant that he and his mother and his father and his grandparents on his mother's side and his brother and his sister and her husband and their one-year-old baby all lived together in a one-bedroom apartment. Life was hell for the Czarlinskys, to say the least. It may sound like a cliché, but the only form of entertainment and escapism they had, was the bottle.

The Montreal Games was Vladimir's first taste of life beyond the Iron Curtain and he gobbled up everything in sight as if he were starving to death. And on the very first day of practice out on the field, he met and fell head over heels, in more ways than one, for an eighteen-year-old African-American track star named Elmira Hamilton.

Elmira's specialty was the broad jump. Well, Vladimir jumped this broad and the two fell madly in love. He defected to the United States, they were married immediately by a justice of the peace and then settled in Wanton Bluff, North Carolina. It was Elmira's hometown and located just northeast of Ragland.

Never having known her mother, Elmira was the love of her father's life. The only child George Washington Hamilton sired, as far as he knew, she lived with him in a small tobacco worker's house. George was a janitor for the elementary school during the day, and at night he worked the night guard's shift at the American Tobacco Company.

Still, money was tight and times were tough for the Washingtons. And when Vladimir moved in, things turned from bad to worse.

Number one, Vladimir was white. Number two, there wasn't enough room. Number three, George Washington Hamilton accused Vladimir Czarlinsky of being a Communist. Truth is, he was. Number four, Vladimir couldn't speak English. Number five, two months after being married, Elmira dropped dead of a heart attack during a track practice in the heat of that summer.

Devastated and feeling no reason to live, George Washington Hamilton passed away, almost a year to that date, from a broken heart.

Vladimir inherited a small amount of money along with the house, and ended up starting the first taxicab company in that area. He, too, was emotionally destroyed by Elmira's death and never remarried. And although there's no less than a full liter of Russian vodka coursing through his veins at any one time, Vladimir Czarlinsky still had the first American dollar he had ever made and was now the wealthiest citizen of Wanton Bluff.

Outside the airport, Vladimir pulled up to the taxi area,

stopped in front of Lex and popped his trunk open. Vladimir showed no signs of getting out of the car; Lex gave him a look, threw his luggage into the trunk and slammed it shut. He reluctantly got into the backseat.

"Vladimir," he whispered.

He floored the car and glanced at Lex in the rear view mirror.

"You not look so good."

"Gee thanks."

"You want to see new doctor in town? She just treat men. Everybody smiles after. Even me."

Vladimir laughed uncontrollably as Lex shook his head and looked out the window.

*   *   *   *

Junior's car pulled off River Road and onto the long and winding drive up to Terror. For a brief moment Clairese had stopped screaming at Mattie Lee.

Under his breath Junior counted one overgrown tree limb after another, as they reached out with knobby fists and beat against the side of his car.

"One, two, three, four, five, six, seven…eight," he whispered.

Clairese glared at Junior. "Did you say something?"

The counting had become an uncontrollable habit with Junior, brought on by the stress and anxiety that he was living with on a daily basis. Akin to the repetitive actions made by obsessively compulsive people, Junior knew he was a now a bonafide "checker." In fact, he knew that if he drove either up or down the drive to Terror and did not count the beating fists of the tree branches hitting against the side of his car, something terrible, something horrific, something catastrophic, would happen to him.

Their Kelly-green, 1962 Ford Falcon, running on its last legs, inched its way up to the top of the hill and past Terror to the gardener's cottage. A wedding gift from Trudy Lee and Bert, it was originally offered rent-free to them till Junior got his feet on the ground financially. Twelve years later and living from paycheck to paycheck, they were still living in what Trudy Lee affectionately called "The Slaves' Quarters."

"Mattie Lee Martindale? The moment we get into our house you are to wash your mouth out with soap! Is that understood? Then I want you to write a letter of apology to your piano teacher, Mr. Crould. And then you will sit down at our piano and you are not to get up until you play your recital piece perfectly all the way through. Little girls who make wrongful use of the name of the Lord…fry in hell!"

The car came to a stop and Mattie Lee jumped out as her mother opened her door.

"God damn son of a bitch!" Mattie Lee screamed as she ran up onto Terror's back porch.

"Wait till I get my hands on her!" Clairese declared as she struggled out of the car.

Instead of opening the back porch door, Mattie Lee jumped right through the ripped screen. Once inside, she smiled, skipped happily into Trudy Lee's kitchen, and took a hard candy out of a glass jar on the counter. She popped it into her mouth and shoved it up into her cheek. She walked over to the maid's room and looked in.

"Grandpa Bert? Granny Martindale?"

"In the bathroom," Roscoe hollered.

Clairese lumbered up to the screen porch. "It's all Trudy Lee's fault, Junior. You've got to talk to her."

"Ah, come on, Clairese."

"Mattie Lee Martindale!" she hollered.

Her nasal voice scratched at Mattie Lee's eardrums. "Jesus Christ." Thinking fast, she dove onto the loveseat in the keeping room, sobbing hysterically.

Clairese marched into the kitchen followed by Junior. "Did you just say it again?"

"Say what?" she asked sheepishly.

"You cuss like that again and I'll beat the living daylights out of you." Clairese promptly stepped right into the now glue-like uncooked pecan pie mixture on the floor. It was so sticky that it pulled her Mary Jane right off her foot.

"What the...?" She looked down at her foot and Junior bumped into her. "Your mother's house is a pigsty."

"Clairese, calm down," he said as he picked up her shoe.

"I will not calm down. We all know cleanliness is next to Godliness. And she's a bad influence on Mattie Lee."

Junior tore off a paper towel to clean the shoe. "I don't think..."

She grabbed it away from him. "Yes, I know she helps us out enormously, sitting for Mattie Lee, but the price we're paying is much too high." She turned on the kitchen faucet and started scrubbing the faux leather shoe.

Junior started to sweat. "Then..."

"And she's getting worse."

And stutter. "Well..."

"Do I have to remind you of last week?"

And tremble. "No, I remem..."

"Your mother covered our daughter with her war paint and then dropped Mattie Lee off at her Bible class. Father Ken called and asked me to pick her up. He said it was disgraceful, sending a ten-year-old child to the house of the Lord looking like a tart. I've never been so embarrassed. I wouldn't be surprised if the church puts us on probation."

"She..."

"And it took me an hour to scrub her face clean. You know, it wouldn't hurt if Trudy Lee went to church once in a while."

"They..."

"I know! I know! The steeple would probably fall on her, then they would have to close the church and then I would be kicked off the bazaar committee."

"Why…"

"Why it's all perfectly clear to me, now. Trudy Lee is possessed. That's it! Your mother is full of the devil. She should be exorcised."

Roscoe came out of the bathroom drying his hands and looking at the three of them. "Hey, Junior and Clairese." Mattie Lee shifted the hard candy in her mouth to the other cheek and bit her tongue in the process, letting out a cry. "What's with Mattie Lee?"

"Your mother! Mattie Lee got all flustered during her recital and blurted out…swear words."

He fought to suppress a smile. "Like what?"

"Like…like…being a good Christian woman, I can't repeat…"

Trudy Lee came down the back staircase trying to hike up a too tight strapless cocktail dress. "God damn son-of-a-bitch!"

"There! See? It's all her fault," declared Clairese.

"What have I done now?"

Clairese turned to her husband for support. "Junior?"

"Trudy…well, Mattie Lee…she…"

"She blew her piano recital and used the Lord's name in vain. And it's all your fault," accused Clairese.

Mattie Lee cried harder, ran up the back staircase and then stopped to listen. The tips of her shoes could just barely be seen.

"What are you talking about?" Trudy Lee asked as she checked the pie in the oven.

"I heard you. When she was practicing her piece yesterday," continued Clairese. "She stumbled over that hard part and I heard you say, 'That's where it's going to happen, Mattie Lee. You're going to get to this section and choke.'"

"Why I never," Trudy Lee declared while sticking a toothpick into the pecan pie.

"You did too. You said, 'You'll choke and then time will stand still. You'll panic and get flop sweat and you won't know where you are.' And that's just what happened. Mattie Lee choked and now she never wants to play again."

"Fine," laughed Trudy Lee. "She wasn't that good anyway." She slipped the pie back into the oven.

"Junior? Are you going to let her talk about Mattie Lee like that?"

He pulled out a handkerchief and started dabbing at the sweat on his forehead. "Trudy…"

Suddenly, the phone rang.

"Ding, round one," Roscoe whispered sarcastically.

Mattie Lee came back down the stairs as Trudy Lee cleared her throat. Simultaneously, paying no heed to one another, Trudy Lee and Clairese started talking at the same time.

Clairese looked at Junior. "She can't get away with this. I know we wanted to try to recreate a family unity but it's just not working. We should never have moved into the gardener's cottage."

While Trudy Lee topped her. "I bet it's my Lex again. He's the only one who appreciates me in this family. He probably wants to know if I need anything from the store and it's," she glared at Clairese, "the Slaves' Quarters."

She finally picked up the phone. "Hello?...Yes, this is Trudy Lee Martindale...Yes, my mother is Anastasia Battles...Yes, but her flight doesn't get in till..." Suddenly her toned changed dramatically. "Oh, she did?...She what?...Oh, my God!...Was she thrown?...Oh, my God!...Strangled?...Oh, my God!...Could they shut it off?...Yes, yes...I'll be there...Yes."

Stunned, Trudy Lee hung up the phone.

After a moment of silence, Mattie Lee asked innocently, "Is she dead?"

"No. No, of course not. She had an accident on an escalator."

"On a what?" asked Clairese.

"Her heel broke on the escalator at the airport," Trudy Lee said as she went to the wall mirror to check her make-up and fix her hair. "She fell over backwards and couldn't get up. A stranger ran to help her but her scarf got caught in the step. Management shut off the escalator but not till the scarf had done some damage to her throat."

"That's awful," exclaimed Junior.

"And she's blind, too," added Clairese.

"Just legally blind," snapped Trudy Lee. "Serves her right. I told her to let Aunt Verna travel with her. But oh, no, she has to be independent. They've taken her to the hospital."

Trudy Lee grabbed her handbag and coat as they all started to leave.

"Maybe she'll need stitches?" Mattie Lee smiled.

Just then, the toilet flushed. Everyone stopped and looked at each other.

"Junior, you stay with your father," ordered Trudy Lee.

"No! I mean I can't. I mean Grandma Battles might need me."

He ran out through the screen porch door.

"For God's sake, he won't bite you," hollered Trudy Lee.

"I'll stay," offered Roscoe as he went into the maid's room.

"Me too," said Mattie Lee.

Clairese kissed her cheek that she thought was swollen from crying. "All right, but you mind your Uncle Roscoe and no candy. You know how diabetes runs in our blood."

"Roscoe?" shouted Trudy Lee. "Lex's pie comes out in five minutes."

He came out of the bedroom with a rocking chair and took it into the bathroom.

"Roscoe? Did you hear me?"

"Yes, Mother."

She applied yet another layer of lipstick to her heavily painted mouth and then ran out the screen porch door followed by Clairese.

Mattie Lee skipped to the candy jar, took a handful out and shoved them into her pocket. She unwrapped one, popped it into her mouth and looked towards the bathroom.

"Uncle Roscoe?"

Roscoe backed out of the bathroom, pulling the rocker with Bert sitting in it. It slid effortlessly along the rug and into the bedroom. He eased an arm under Bert's legs and another behind his back. "OK, Pop. One, two, three." He lifted Bert onto the bed as Mattie Lee watched and sucked on her candy.

Out in the driveway, Junior had already started his car and was nervously revving the engine.

"Damn it," Trudy Lee swore. "I wanted to be here when Lex arrived."

"He isn't bringing that friend with him, is he?" asked Clairese.

"Don't you dare," warned Trudy Lee.

"I love Lex. I just don't want my Mattie Lee being…affected by his lifestyle."

"Don't worry, dear. We're leaving that up to you."

Clairese opened the passenger's door but Trudy Lee slipped in and slammed it shut.

"Full of the devil," Clairese declared as she got into the back seat.

Junior floored the car and they tore down the driveway.

"One, two, three, four, five, six, seven, eight," he shouted.

"Junior, what in God's name are you counting?" asked Trudy Lee.

"Beating fists," he answered cryptically.

"Slow down," screamed Clairese. "We're going to have an accident."

Junior's car sped out of the driveway and without any of them noticing, passed Lex coming in from the airport.

"I drop you off here," Vladimir insisted as he stopped the car on River Road.

Lex coughed from the alcoholic fumes emanating from Vladimir's body. "But it's like a quarter of a mile up to my house."

"Last time I take you up and the time before, trees scratch my cab. Paint all ruined."

"But I'm paying you to drive me home."

"I not go up. That is final!" Vladimir got out of his car, opened his trunk and threw Lex's bag onto the gravel. "$15.50."

"It's highway robbery," Lex screamed as a car zoomed by, almost hitting them. He gave Vladimir exactly $15.50.

"No tip?"

"No tip! You do your job and I'll tip. Otherwise, suffer the consequences."

"Kak auknetsia, tak i otkliknetsia!" shouted Vladimir vehemently. Translation: curses, like chickens, come home to roost.

Little did Lex know how appropriate Vladimir's threat was. The Russian then flicked his hand out at Lex, jumped back into his car and sped off.

"The one and only cab driver in Ragland. I'm going to regret having done that."

Lex grabbed his bag and walked up to their mailbox. He put the flag down and took out the mail. He then moved a trash can aside that was resting on a small bed of tulips and tried to perk up the flowers.

At that moment, Delbert Lovejoy, who lived next door to the Martindales, peeled out of his driveway in his pick-up truck, just missing Lex. He slammed on his brakes and stuck his head out of the window.

"Hey, faggot! Home from the big city?"

Delbert was Ragland's resident redneck and Lex's nemesis. He was also as big as he was stupid. When they were small children Delbert had taken an immediate and intense dislike to Lex. But Lex managed to steer clear of this oaf's path for the most part because he could run faster. But even though Delbert was four years Lex's senior, he was held back in third grade four years in a row. Sharing the same classes from then on, Delbert strived to make every following year in grade school, junior high and high school a living hell for Lex. One of the worst moments was when Delbert had caught Lex kissing Chucky Puglisi in the eighth-grade boys' bathroom. Twenty-one years later and Delbert still wouldn't let him live it down.

At age sixteen, Delbert had got seventeen-year-old Betsy Mantle pregnant. Betsy Mantle aka Betsy Metal. Unlike most American towns, Ragland had its annual Homecoming over Thanksgiving weekend. On rare occasions, a few people who had left this Southern town after high school would return to celebrate the holiday with family and friends, and cheer on the seasonal football game. Actually, Ragland High's football team was so pathetic most came to cheer on the cheerleaders. And the leader of the pack was none other than Betsy Mantle.

Betsy was beautiful. Betsy was stacked. And the only thing Betsy Mantle liked more than cheerleading was partying. Drinking in particular.

In her junior year of high school it was a surprise to no one that Betsy Mantle was crowned Homecoming Queen. And to celebrate after the football game that Ragland High lost, and after a stuffing of Thanksgiving dinner, she and her best girlfriends, Gloria Lynn Lutter and June Stump, proceeded to indulge in Betsy's beverage of choice, gin and Fresca.

Having stolen a bottle of Betsy's mother's gin and consumed it while sitting in the school's parking lot, the girls decided to raid Gloria Lynn Lutter's mother's liquor cabinet. With June Stump driving and Gloria Lynn sitting in the middle, Betsy hung her tiara-adorned head out of the red mustang convertible as they tore down Copperhead Road.

"Hello residents of Ragland, North Carolina!" Betsy slurred. "Bow down to your royal highness! Respect my presence and know your places!"

Gloria Lynn and June Stump laughed with glee.

"No applause, you peons!" shouted Betsy. "Just money!"

And whether it was poor judgment due to alcohol or hydroplaning due to rain, June Stump miscalculated the turn onto Blossom Street and came a little too close to a telephone pole and nicked the side of Betsy Mantle's head.

Betsy said she couldn't remember any of the accident, nor the three-month coma she was hurtled into. But it took a doctor's buzz saw to remove the tiara from her skull and they promptly replaced it with a titanium plate.

Betsy Metal, just never was the same. In fact, people in Ragland said she must have been out of her mind to marry Delbert Lovejoy. Well, out of the mind she had left.

After Delbert managed to get her pregnant, they married the following year and moved in with Delbert's parents. They continued to live there and have more and more children. The last count was eleven. Six girls and five boys. And to Lex's delight each one of them had something wrong. Some had too many fingers or toes. Several were wall-eyed with either their left, right or both eyes veering outwards. And none of them could read, write, or count past the number ten, confirming Lex's theory that Betsy must be a close relative of Delbert's. Hopefully, his long lost sister.

"You gonna have a date with Chucky Puglisi tonight, lover boy?" Delbert spat in Lex's direction and then sped off down River Road.

As soon as he was out of hearing distance, Lex safely yelled back, "Fuck you, moron!"

He started up the long driveway to his house. He wondered how many times the school bus had dropped him off? How many times he had missed the school bus? How many times had Bert or Trudy Lee forgotten to pick him up at a sports or school event and he had ended up walking home?

In the early years, taking care of the front lawn, as well as the rest of the grounds, was his chore. Not that it was asked of him. No one else would do it. But he loved the job just the same. Instant results he found incredibly satisfying. But once he went off to college no one tended to the property, and Trudy Lee adopted what she called the naturalist's approach to gardening. She just let everything grow wild.

Halfway up the drive he spotted a dilapidated tree house he had built when he couldn't have been much older than Mattie Lee. He stepped over some dead branches and touched the silver, weathered two-by-fours he had tapped into the tree to make a ladder.

Behind it he saw a deflated inner tube, the huge kind used for tractor-trailer trucks. Lex picked it up and his mind flashed back to the first time he remembered playing with it.

* * * *

It was the summer of '59 and Lex was four years old. To escape the suffocating heat and humidity, Trudy Lee threw him, Mona Lee and Junior into their mauve-colored Ford station wagon and headed to Pomp's Pond.

Peyton Pomp was Ragland's most infamous Mayor. Serving from 1948 to 1956, he managed to turn this thriving community, which was financially operating in the black, into a depressed, Federally dependent eyesore by personally embezzling every cent the town owned. He also deceptively and illegally persuaded resident tobacco growers to sell their land to the American Tobacco Company for one penny on the dollar, pocketing a huge take on the deal, then jumped onto a plane to Belize and was never heard of again.

Tops in his class, Bert Martindale was recruited right out of college, as a chemist, by the American Tobacco Company. Attracting him with salaries and incentives that never came through, Bert's job was to create the most addictive, yet tasty, cigarette on the market. Formaldehyde, cyanide and nicotine were the chemicals of choice.

It was sad but fitting that Bert was dying from his own creations. And it wasn't till decades later that researchers discovered that the high rates of liver, kidney and pancreatic cancer in Ragland were linked to trace levels of these chemicals that had leached into the town's water supply. So, in a roundabout way, it was perfect that Pomp's Pond, which sat out on the back twenty acres of the American Tobacco Company's property, was named after a poisonous politician.

Before the days of children's car seats, Trudy Lee sat Mona Lee and Junior down in the back seat and then put the heavy beach cooler on their laps to keep them strapped down. Full of bologna sandwiches made on white bread with mayonnaise and pickle relish, cold bottles of Tab and brown bags stuffed with ripe plums and peaches, they were trapped till they arrived at the town watering hole.

Even at eight years old, Mona Lee was combative.

"I'm not going into the Polio Pit," she declared. "Carla Wormwood came out of it last week with bloodsuckers on her legs!"

"Suit yourself," Trudy Lee said.

Junior squirmed underneath the cooler. "I can't feel my legs."

Trudy Lee squinted at Lex in the rear view mirror. "Is your brother OK back there?"

Mona Lee turned around and giggled, "Yes, Mother. He's fine."

Seated in the middle of the black inner tube, Lex had proceeded to take every bit of clothing off his body and was throwing them out the back window of the station wagon, piece by piece.

Stopped at a red light, Ludlow's Carpet and Tile truck pulled up beside them.

Mona Lee looked out the window. "Is that gross Mr. Ludlow?"

Trudy Lee quickly checked her hair and make-up in the mirror and then looked across the lane.

"Hi Frank," she purred.

"Afternoon, Trudy Lee. Off to Pomp's?"

"You got it," she winked. "The linoleum in my kitchen looks swell."

"Glad you like it," Frank blushed.

"Will you be making an appearance in your swimming attire?"

"Have a delivery to make over in Methuen. Guess I could swing around on my way back. But I don't have a suit with me."

"You could always skinny dip," Trudy Lee laughed.

Frank blushed, again. The light changed and he sped off as Mona Lee stuck her tongue out at him.

"He's so disgusting, Mother."

"I can't feel my feet," complained Junior.

Trudy Lee headed down the road humming to herself. From behind you could see Lex smiling and dropping his bathing suit out the rear window.

Once they arrived at Pomp's Pond, the children basically had to fend for themselves. Trudy Lee plopped her beach chair down into the mud as Lex and Mona Lee ran to the edge of the water. Still trying to bring back circulation to his legs, Junior limped out of the station wagon and sat down next to Trudy Lee. All the other mothers waved and gossiped while their children stood at the edge of the pond, hesitating to go in.

It was a smallish, man-made watering hole and beyond you could see the ominous American Tobacco Company and its huge smokestacks burping out black smoke. Drainpipes emptied waste at the far end of the shore.

Mona Lee stuck her toe into the greenish-yellow stagnant water. "I'll give you a quarter to go into the Polio Pit, Lex."

"OK."

She threw the inner tube into the pond and then placed Lex on top of it and then pushed him out. Mona Lee promptly left him. He spun around several times and then quietly slipped into the slimy pond.

Constantly looking around to see if Frank had arrived, Trudy Lee had no idea that Lex was gone. It was Lorraine Ludlow, of all people, who ran to the water's edge, hesitated and then waded out to the inner tube and dragged Lex back up to the surface.

Coughing water out of his lungs and covered in leeches, Lorraine dropped Lex at Trudy Lee's feet. "Your kid almost drowned and keep your God damn fucking hands off of my husband!"

"Whatever are you talking about?" laughed Trudy Lee as Lorraine stomped away. She then turned to Lex and picked the bloodsuckers off him as if they were daisies in a field. "Darling, I know you love the water, but you could drown in a cup of tea. And where's your bathing suit?"

Lex, Junior and Mona Lee never saw Frank Ludlow at the house again. However, eight months later, Roscoe was born. It seems as though Frank had laid more than just Trudy Lee's linoleum.

*   *   *   *

Back in the present, Lex dropped the huge black inner tube and walked farther up the driveway until he found the world's largest dog bone. A huge smile came across his face.

"Bob?" Lex shouted. "Here, Bob! Come on, boy!" He waited, hoping the dog would come running down the driveway, as he used to when he was a pup. Even though Lex knew Bob had already far surpassed his expiration date and had lost his hearing and most of his eyesight, he couldn't help but hope. He threw the big bone down on the side of the drive and continued up the hill.

Out of breath, Lex stood in front of the massive house, soaking everything in. Even though the columns supporting the veranda were rotting at their bases, the paint on the window shutters was peeling and the transom window above the front door had a crack in it, he still loved this pseudo southern belle. He turned around and looked out over the front lawn. New York might be where he lived now, but Ragland, like it or not, was and always would be his home. Lex took a deep breath of North Carolinian air, coughed and then entered the house.

THREE

LIKE FATHER, LIKE SON

Lex was probably the only Martindale who used the front door. Not that he was against entering from the rear. Coming in through the main entrance always felt more dramatic and grand to him.

Knowing it was always unlocked, he struggled with the door-knob and then hip-checked it open. He dropped his bag in the front hallway, listening.

"Hel-looo?" Lex peeped into the parlor and then into the dining room. "Hel-looo!" He looked up the front staircase. "Mother?"

Feeling a bit deflated, he walked down the hallway to the kitchen. "I'm here." He opened the oven and smelled the pie. "Anybody home?"

Mattie Lee burst out of the maid's room and ran to Lex.

"Uncle Tappy Toes!"

"Mattie Lee," he squealed, picking her up.

She immediately examined his neck. "You have a rash."

"Nothing gets by you, does it?" he laughed setting her back down.

"I had my first piano recital and I really screwed up bad, on purpose. Your mother gave me the idea. And now I don't think I have to take lessons anymore."

"But you'll play for me, won't you? I bet you're wonderful."

She popped a hard candy into her mouth. "No, I'm really bad. Trudy Lee says I lack digital prosperity."

"I think that's dexterity," Lex laughed. "Where is everyone?"

"They've all gone to rescue Grandma Battles. She was eaten by an escalator."

"She what?"

Roscoe came out of the maid's room. "Hey."

"Hi, Rosc." Lex tried to embrace him but Roscoe coldly stood before him with his arms pinned to his sides. Recognizing the iciness, Lex stepped away. "So, do you miss the North Pole?"

Roscoe walked over to the kitchen sink and washed his hands. "I miss the money. I was bartending at the most popular bar and if I hadn't come home to help with Dad, I could easily have made a few hundred thousand by now."

Lex actually let out a little laugh. "You were making that much?"

"Yeah, that much," he said defensively. "But some of us put family before career."

Lex was at a total loss as to how to handle Roscoe. "How is Trudy Lee dealing with everything?"

Mattie Lee sensed the tension between her uncles. "My mother says she's full of the devil and should be circumcised."

The brothers shared a laugh and then an uncomfortable silence as Mattie Lee went over to the old record collection by the stereo.

"So, how is Dad?" Feeling guilty, Lex rambled on. "I would have come sooner but I've been tied up with re-writes of my book proposal and money's been tight and..."

"Lex, we almost lost him last night."

"What happened?"

Roscoe went to the refrigerator and pulled out a carton of

milk. "Mother and I were walking him to the bathroom and he collapsed. We called the doctor but by the time he got here, Dad had rallied back." He started drinking straight from the carton.

"He always was stubborn."

He gulped down half the container and then wiped his mouth. "The doctor said any other person would have died a month ago."

Lex looked over at the maid's room. "Gosh, so how is he now?"

"See for yourself. He should be asleep."

Lex walked over to the bedroom doorway, hesitated and then entered the room.

The shades were drawn and Bert was asleep on his side with his back to the door. Tentatively, Lex walked towards the bed, staring at his father.

"Dad?" he asked in a quiet whisper. Lex walked closer and stood next to the bed. He turned on the light sitting on the night-stand. "Dad?"

Lex reached out and softly touched his father's shoulder. It felt as if there was no flesh on his bones. Still asleep, Bert let out a feeble sigh and rolled onto his back.

Lex was horrified. For a split second, he saw his own face on his father's body; drawn, gaunt, emaciated. He blinked and stumbled backwards, hitting the bedroom wall. He stared again at Bert's face, and then rushed out of the room.

He slid down onto a hardback chair in the hallway, forcing himself to breathe. He thought he should cry. He wanted to cry, but no tears appeared. Time stood still as his mind raced back to a one o'clock appointment he'd had with his doctor almost three months earlier.

*　*　*　*

Being self-employed and in light of Bert's first diagnosis of cancer, Lex thought the responsible thing for him to finally do would be to get a life insurance policy. At least that's what he told Peter.

But in truth, Lex wasn't feeling his normal self. Since he was a young child he had suffered from classic migraines, which included vomiting. But they were happening much more frequently now. Actually, on a weekly basis. And he hid from Peter, his hypochondriac lover, his recent bouts of chills, fevers and flu-like symptoms. Even the night sweats he wrote off to working out too hard at the gym.

"Lex, you don't have to do this," reminded Peter.

"But I want life insurance and I don't want that company testing me."

"Why life insurance now? You're not in debt. I don't need the money."

"Because...because...," Lex felt cornered. Trapped. "Because I want to be sure."

"But you've been tested before and I'm negative too. Why would it change now?"

Lex didn't answer and didn't look up at him. His silence spoke for itself. Lex grabbed his coat and ran out of the apartment. He took the express train from the Upper West Side of Manhattan down to 42nd Street, where he transferred to an N train to get to Sharon's office.

Sitting in her waiting room were four other gay men. Well, he thought four.

Paul, the receptionist, put down his phone. "Karen? You can go back and Michael will do your bloods."

And with that, the fourth man, a lesbian, got up and marched back to the lab.

Sharon was a brilliant doctor and a lesbian herself. Therefore she attracted a large clientele of gay people.

Paul called out again. "Lex?"

"Yes?" he replied a little too loud.

"Sharon will see you now."

"OK," he shouted even louder.

He broke out into flop sweat and felt the room beginning to

spin as he stood up.

"You OK?" Paul asked in a concerned voice. Always overly officious to say the least, he seemed alarmingly kind today.

"Yup," Lex whispered with caution.

He sat in Sharon's examining room for what seemed like forever. Lex believed in and practiced safe sex. And although he was never one for "stranger" sex, he had experienced an incredible and erotic connection with a man about nine months earlier. It was nothing important but completely lustful. They had eyed each other on a subway and without speaking a word, Lex had got off the train in the west 20's and followed the man to his apartment. Very few words were spoken, passion was at its highest. But when the quick but intense rendezvous was over, Lex was horrified to discover that the man's condom had broken.

Sharon finally appeared at the door. "Hi sweetie," she said, her voice much higher than usual.

Not only had he been a patient of hers for over ten years but they had also become close friends socially. This was mainly because they both bowled for the gay bowling league.

"So, what's the prognosis, doctor?" he asked in his best Bette Davis imitation from Dark Victory.

She sat down without looking at him and her eyes welled up with tears.

Lex knew. She didn't have to say a word.

They both sat there in silence. Lex started to tremble. He thought he should cry. He wanted to cry. But no tears. She on the other hand, fell apart.

"I'm so sorry, Lex," she sobbed.

The innate caretaker in him took over. That he had tested positive for the AIDS virus didn't surprise him. However, this didn't mean that he wasn't frightened to death. And to control the overwhelming sense of terror that was brewing in his body, Lex threw his attention onto his doctor.

"I'll be OK, Sharon."

"This is so unprofessional of me," she said as she wiped away her tears.

"I think it's flattering," Lex laughed. "I was ready for this. In fact, I would have been shocked if I had tested negative."

"Lex," she said gravely, "you're not HIV positive."

For a moment he was speechless.

"I'm not?" A huge smile of relief appeared on his face.

"No."

"Oh my God! That's incredible. Here I was so sure..."

Sharon started to cry, again.

"Sharon?"

She blew her nose and gained her composure.

"Lex. You have leukemia."

"I what?"

"Cancer of the blood."

"Cancer?" He couldn't breathe.

"We need to do more tests to define what kind you have."

"But this can't...be."

"Your increased problems with headaches and vomiting probably indicate acute leukemia of the central nervous system. And the tiny red spots under your skin we looked at are called petechiae, another symptom of leukemia. I'm going to send you to an oncologist, a hematologist and a pathologist."

"Why so many?" he asked in a little boy voice.

"I want to be very conservative. I don't want to miss anything. We'll do a spinal tap which will tell us whether or not the leukemia cells are in the fluid that fills the spaces in and around your brain and spinal cord."

"But how could this happen to me?"

"Lex, there are so many variables. But one cause we see popping up more frequently is exposure to toxic chemicals. Benzene, methanol, formaldehyde."

Then it dawned on Lex. "God damn fucking Pomp's Pond."

"Pomp's what?" asked Sharon.

"Doesn't matter. Ah shit."

"I want to do some x-rays, cat scans and...I'm going to set you up for a bone marrow aspiration."

"Why?" he asked, frightened.

"I want to cover all bases. We need to check a sample of bone marrow under a microscope."

The thought of their removing bone marrow made Lex weak in the knees. "What if it is this...acute...version?"

"Our hopes are better. Symptoms and the disease progress more quickly than the chronic type; however the odds we lick this are on our side. Chronic is very hard to manage."

"Then I'll take the acute version, please?" he asked trying to lighten things up.

They sat there in silence.

"Will I have to do chemotherapy?"

"Sooner than later. Probably intravenously. We blast the body, then let you rest."

"Side effects?"

"It's so individual, Lex."

"My hair."

"Most likely. But it will grow back. During the cycles of treatment your immune system might weaken. Literally, stay away from sick people. And don't stress yourself."

"Don't stress yourself," he said to himself sarcastically.

"I need to send you over to the specialists now."

Lex got up and walked to the window. It was a gorgeous winter day. Everyone down on the sidewalk seemed so busy passing by. So directed. Lex examined face after face. Each one looked so happy. So content. So healthy.

"Lex, do you want me to call Peter?"

"No. I just need...I just need to..." he opened up the window. "I just need to keep breathing."

"I'm sorry, Lex."

"Sharon, the night before the test, Peter and I drank an awful lot of wine. Do you think that could have had a bearing on the test results?"

The moment the question came out of his mouth, Lex heard how stupid it sounded. How desperate.

"I'm afraid not."

There was a lengthy pause.

"Sharon? How long are we talking?"

She reached out for his hand. "Lex, we have to take this one step at a time. And it's the quality of life that we should focus in on right now."

Lex felt a lump form in his throat.

"You OK?" she asked.

He didn't respond.

*　*　*　*

"You OK?" Roscoe called out. "Lex?"

"Yes. Yes." Lex pulled himself together. Looking as though he had seen a ghost, he walked back into the kitchen.

Roscoe held up a tin-measuring cup. "Dad's been having bursts of energy and getting up and out of bed on his own. I think he calls for Mom and me but we can't hear him. I'm going to tie this to his bed. He can bang it when he wants us."

There was a moment of awkward silence as Roscoe pulled some string out of a junk drawer and threaded it thru the handle of the cup.

Lex finally spoke. "It doesn't even look like him."

"He stopped eating. He refuses a feeding tube, medication and painkillers."

"But he must be in pain."

"Probably."

"Well, what does he say?"

"Lex, the man has cancer of the throat. Not to mention his lungs, heart, liver and lymph. He can't talk now. Not that he ever did before."

"Well, whose idea was it to take him out of the hospital?"

Lex turned on the sink faucet and started splashing water on his face.

"His. He wants to die at home."

Lex dried his face and looked sincerely at his brother. "My God. I didn't know, Roscoe. Mother said it was bad but I thought she was being melodramatic. Has Junior been helping out?"

"No. Something's going on. I don't know what it is but he's different. Our big, strong, older brother is a wimp. The sight of Dad dying makes him fall apart."

Lex almost put his hand on Roscoe's shoulder and then chose not to. "How are you doing?"

"I'm so darned tired I really don't feel anything anymore. He sleeps thirty to forty-five minutes at a time, then he wants to go to the bathroom."

"Rosc, I'm surprised he doesn't have a catheter?"

"He does but he keeps pulling it out. As long as he can get to the bathroom, have some beer and a cigarette, he knows he's still alive."

"Isn't it ironic? That's what's killing him."

"It's called suicide, Lex."

Lex turned away to check where Mattie Lee was. Seeing that she was engrossed with records, he turned back to his brother. "But why, Roscoe, why?"

"Why didn't he and Mom divorce forty years ago and live happily ever after? Why didn't he quit the job at the plant and follow his dream of becoming a track coach? Why did he stop being a father before I was even born?"

"No, Rosc. Why did you come back?"

Mattie Lee came running into the kitchen with a record in her hand.

"You ready, Uncle Tappy Toes?"

"You bet."

She ran back into the keeping room and slipped the LP onto the turntable.

Roscoe pulled him to the side. "Lex, I have to ask you this."

"What?"

"Can you be on duty tonight? I know it's your birthday and all but if I don't have a break and some sleep, I think I'm going to blow a circuit."

"I guess so. If you show me what to do."

Mattie Lee pushed the loveseat out of the way and then dragged Lex over to the hard floor.

"Let's dance!"

Out of the speakers emerged a very old tap dancing rendition of *Tea For Two*. They began their routine, obviously one they both knew very well. Neither of them had rhythm, causing the dance to look awkward and off-sync. It appeared funny, but charming at the same time.

Meanwhile Roscoe went into Bert's room with the measuring cup, string and a cold, wet facecloth. Bert opened his eyes.

"Hey, Pop."

Bert blinked as Roscoe put the facecloth onto his forehead.

"Yeah, Lex is here."

Bert smiled as Roscoe tied the cup to his bed.

"If you need anything, Pop, just bang the cup. OK?"

Bert blinked his eyes.

Roscoe came back out into the keeping room just in time for the finish of their dance. He applauded as Mattie Lee and Lex fell down onto the floor laughing.

"Bravo," cheered Roscoe. "You two are…different."

Lex started to rub his forehead.

"You OK, Uncle Lex?" asked Mattie Lee.

Roscoe studied his face. "Yeah, you look a little flushed."

"You would be too after that number." He got up off the floor and then noticed what was lined up along the fireplace mantel. "My God, I wondered what had happened to all these awful pictures of me."

"Don't let it go to your head," laughed Roscoe. "They go up the day you come home."

Mattie Lee looked up at Lex as he squeezed the back of his neck.

"Are you getting one of your awful migraines, Uncle Lex?"

"No, honey. I'm fine as long as I stay away from stress, bright lights and meat."

Mattie Lee and Roscoe looked at each other.

"She didn't."

Roscoe laughed. "Every year she makes your favorite, Lex."

"But I hate crown roast of pork."

Mattie Lee opened the refrigerator and looked in. "She says this one's fit for a king."

"Or a queen," Roscoe whispered under his breath with an evil grin.

Lex gave him a hard glare. "What's wrong with her brain?"

"Speaking of which," exclaimed Roscoe, "do you remember Mr. Bisbee?"

Lex's mind raced back to junior high. "You mean the three-hundred-and-fifty-pound shop teacher who was always trying to touch us boys while working the drill press?"

"Yeah! They found out it was because of a brain tumor and they took it out and now he's normal."

For a split second Lex thought Roscoe knew of his cancer. But then seeing him and Mattie Lee laugh hysterically, he realized it was just a coincidence and he quickly joined in.

"Noooo!" laughed Lex. "Roscoe, remember Mrs. Steinman the science teacher? When she was mad she'd wave that shrunken arm at you."

He grabbed Lex's arm. "Or how about Mrs. La Medici. She had no arm!"

They all doubled over with laughter.

When Lex managed to catch his breath he glanced down at

the kitchen floor. "Hey, where's Bob's dish?"

Mattie Lee and Roscoe looked at each other.

Very gently Mattie Lee said, "Bob's gone."

"He ran away again?"

"No, Lex," Roscoe said. "Um, Bob died."

Stunned, Lex searched for words. "Why didn't anyone tell me?"

Roscoe continued. "It just happened last night. Mother was making us watch some dumb-ass movie with Marilyn Monroe and Bob died on the rug right over there." He pointed to a large stain on the threadbare Oriental. "Real quiet like. He didn't suffer at all. We thought you'd like to see him before we buried him. He's out in he garage."

"My dog, Bob, is dead?" Finally, emotionally breaking down, Lex ran out through the screen porch.

Smoke suddenly appeared in the kitchen.

"Uncle Roscoe," screamed Mattie Lee, "the pie!"

Roscoe grabbed a mitt, ran to the oven, opened it and a tremendous cloud of smoke billowed out. He took the pie out, which looked like a blackened Frisbee, and threw it into the sink.

"Mattie Lee, I think I'm cooked."

FOUR

TINY STINGING INSECTS THAT TORMENT EXPOSED FLESH

Lex tripped over a garden hose that was tangled up on the floor of the garage and fell to his knee.

"Damn," he shouted, rubbing it. He got up and looked at the mess. The garage now housed every misplaced thing the Martindales owned except the cars. He actually had to look around to find Bob.

He found him lying on the back workbench on top of a plastic bag. Lex walked slowly over to him. A black mutt, the hair on Bob's face had turned all silver. He'd also lost most of his teeth and one eye was blind and milky white. Lex touched his matted fur and then it happened. The floodgates opened up and Lex burst into tears, irrepressible tears that drenched the dead dog.

Roscoe gave Lex some time to be alone with Bob before joining him in the garage.

"Hey," he whispered quietly.

"Hey." Embarrassed to be seen crying, Lex quickly wiped his tears away. "I just wanted to say goodbye to him." And suddenly Lex started to cry again. Uncontrollable blubbering. "I'm sorry,

Roscoe. You probably think I'm being stupid."

"Lex?" Roscoe searched for the right words. "Bob was a...pain in the ass."

"Don't talk about my dog like that!"

"Your dog?"

"I'm the one who found him tied up at the dump and brought him home and washed him up and fed him."

"Yes and then you moved to New York City. You were a stranger to him. He never acknowledged you. He never came to you when you called him. And he bit you more than any of the rest of us."

Lex unconsciously touched his thigh. "Well, I only had to get shots and stitches once."

"Everyone hated him. He even pushed Mattie Lee down knocking her front tooth out. Clairese tried to poison him."

"No way."

The two brothers stared at each other and then started to laugh.

"Yes. Face it Lex, Bob was a bastard."

"Then why am I so upset?"

"Probably because everything around this fucking place is breaking down and dying."

Roscoe hit so close to home. There was a moment when Lex was tempted to tell him of his own problem and then it passed.

"Maybe," is all Lex mumbled.

Although both Martindale men were close enough to embrace and sensed it would be the supportive thing to do, it would have been much too intimate. So instead, Lex blew his nose while Roscoe nudged a half empty paint can with his boot. He looked over at Bob.

"Geez, he must be older than dirt."

"He sure smells it," Lex laughed as he wiped his face. "Come on. Let's go bury the little shit out back."

Lex threw a blanket over the dog as Roscoe grabbed a shovel.

They opened the garage door and looked out.

"Perfect," Roscoe said sarcastically. "It's raining."

"Let's bury him way out back."

* * * *

Junior's car barreled down Route 1, back to Terror. Wearing a neck brace, Anastasia sat between him and Trudy Lee. Clairese was delegated to the backseat once again, buried beneath luggage.

Anastasia shook her head. "Trudy Lee, why in God's name would I fake a fall like that?"

Trudy Lee looked at her watch and then drummed her fingernails on the vinyl-covered interior. "Honestly, Mother, your obsessive-compulsive need for attention is socially unacceptable."

Anastasia let out a gasp. "My need?"

Clairese's hand emerged from the luggage and grabbed the back of Junior's shirt collar. "Hey mister, where's the fire?"

"I have to get back to the office and…"

Clairese cut him off. "No you don't."

He turned around yelling at the luggage. "Yes, I do! It's tax time!"

"Watch out, Junior," screamed Trudy Lee. "There's a red light."

He jammed on the brakes, just missing the car in front of them, and causing them all to lurch forward. Suddenly, the light turned green and he floored the gas pedal and they all were pressed against their seats. A car crossed in front of him at the intersection and he jammed on the brakes again, jerking them forward.

"Ahhh!" cried Anastasia. "Junior, what did you do, go to Whiplash Auto School?"

"We're all going to need neck braces," Trudy Lee yelled, rubbing her neck.

"Your mother is right, Junior," they heard Clairese mumble.

"Keep driving like this and you'll ruin the clutch."

Anastasia shouted out to her. "Clairese?"

"Yes, Grandma Battles?"

"The only thing you know how to drive is someone crazy."

Junior started counting. "One, one-thousand, two, one-thousand, three, one-thousand, four!" He floored the car again.

"Oh, shit!" shouted Anastasia holding her neck.

*　*　*　*

The rain had just tapered off as Junior's Falcon chugged up the drive and sputtered to a halt at the back of the house. He jumped out and ran around to Trudy Lee's side. After three attempts he was able to open the rusted door. As Trudy Lee stepped out, Anastasia slid across the seat and was about to walk on her own, when Junior slipped his arms around her and lifted her out of the car precariously.

"For God's sake, put me down Junior. I'm not crippled," she groaned, wrestling with him.

Trudy Lee ran to the back porch while primping her hair. "Now Mother, you heard the doctor. No strenuous activity."

"Walking isn't strenuous," she insisted, as the three of them headed for the screen porch.

From underneath Anastasia's luggage, Clairese managed to shout out, "Hey!"

Mattie Lee was looking at album covers in the keeping room when she heard them entering the screen porch. She leaped to her feet and spat her hard candy out into the fireplace, which created a very loud ping.

Junior entered carrying Anastasia followed by Trudy Lee with her big purse.

"Here, Junior. Sit Mother down onto the loveseat."

Exhausted, Junior dropped her down roughly.

"Easy Junior. She's just had an awful ordeal. Now remember,

Mother, the doctor said, 'Don't fall asleep.' You have to stay awake for several hours, and if you vomit, that confirms the concussion."

"Oh mute it, Trudy."

"All right, go ahead and fall asleep. Have a coma! Excuse me for caring." Trudy Lee looked into the oven and then around the kitchen area. "Where's Lex's pecan pie? Where did it go?"

Thinking quickly Mattie Lee said, "Uh, Uncle Roscoe thought it would cool better out in the garage?"

"With Bob?" screamed Trudy Lee.

"No. Bob was getting a little ripe so he and Uncle Lex are burying him out by the old beech tree."

"My Lex is here? Why didn't you tell me?" Trudy Lee ran to the mirror checking her hair and make-up.

"Is that you, Mattie Lee?" asked Grandma Battles.

Clairese finally teetered in, just barely able to carry all of Anastasia's luggage.

"Yup."

"Then come give your Great Granny a big kiss."

As Mattie Lee kissed her, Trudy Lee applied more lipstick.

"Trudy Lee," exclaimed Anastasia, "you look like a tramp with all that make-up."

She continued to study herself in the mirror as she raised her hand, waving as though she were swatting at gnats. "How would you know? You can't see."

"I can hear you layering it on."

Trudy Lee spun around. "Keep it up and I'm sending you back to Detroit, Mother."

"Good."

"Look, you two," said Clairese. "You're at it already."

"Shut up, Clairese!" Trudy Lee and Anastasia shouted in unison.

Trudy Lee ran to the kitchen window displaying dozens of antique, colored-glass bottles that the family had discovered on the property over the years. Some were amber, others cobalt blue. One was even in the shape of a bowling ball. She peeked up and down, in and out. Finally, moving her favorite ruby-colored bottle that she now referred to as the "crying glass" because Roscoe had broken it practicing his swing in the house, she was able to make out her favorite one.

"Oh there he is. I can see my Lex."

Clairese looked over Trudy Lee's shoulder. "My, dressed all in black. You sure can tell he's from New York."

"Manhattan," Trudy Lee said spinning around. "Lex is from Manhattan."

Grabbing umbrellas, she ran out through the screen porch followed by Mattie Lee and Clairese. Junior scooped Anastasia back up into his arms.

"Oh shit," she cried.

Trudy Lee leaped off the porch followed by the others.

"Lex, darling," she shouted.

Across the back property, they all ran to the big old beech tree where Lex and Roscoe were just finishing up with Bob.

"Gird your loins, Lex," warned his brother. "Here comes Mother in the lead."

Lex forced a smile as Trudy Lee ran across Bob's grave in her high heels. Lex pulled her to the side and she threw her arms around him. Roscoe smoothed the dirt over the grave as Trudy Lee gave Lex a huge kiss, smearing lipstick all over his cheek.

"You look so great, dear."

"So do you, Mother."

"No I don't. I look awful." She looked down at Lex's muddy shoes. "Gucci, dear?"

"No, they were Prada."

"Thank God you have my good taste." She kissed him again as Roscoe rolled his eyes and Mattie Lee, Clairese and Junior, carrying Anastasia, caught up to them.

"Hello Lex," panted Clairese. "You've lost weight."

"Hi Clair…"

"I've lost weight," Trudy Lee said, cutting him off. She touched her temple with her fingertips and pulled her face. "But I still look fat. I'm going to lose a few more and then have my face lifted."

"Hate to see what's under it," cackled Anastasia.

Everyone but Trudy Lee laughed.

"Very funny, Mother."

Lex gave Anastasia an awkward kiss as Junior trembled holding her. "Grandma, I hear you fell for some cute guy with great buns on an escalator."

"You got it, Lex. Happy Birthday, dear."

Trudy Lee pulled him away from her. "Come Lex, we must let Mother sleep."

She put her arm through Lex's and headed back to the house as Roscoe, Clairese, Mattie Lee and Junior, carrying Anastasia, followed them.

"Hey," shouted Junior, all out of breath. "Happy Birthday, little brother. Hear your book is doing great. Bestseller list next week?"

Suddenly, Trudy Lee bolted from Lex and made a dash for the house.

"Mother?" Lex shouted.

She looked back once before disappearing into the back porch.

Anastasia started squirming in Junior's arms. "Where's the Midge?"

Lex spun around to look at her. "Oh Grandma, please don't call her that."

Mattie Lee caught up to Lex and squeezed his hand. "What is a midge?"

* * * *

Trudy Lee had thrown on her apron and was feeling the edge of a very large knife. "Dull as a box of hair." She pulled out a fourteen-inch sharpening steel from a drawer and forcefully ran the knife down it.

At this stage in her life, Trudy Lee was sick to death of cooking. Actually, she was tired of coming up with delicious and inventive twists on old family favorites and then watching everyone turn their noses up at them, or come so late to the table that supper was so cold even the dog wouldn't eat it. And more times than not, she would end up having to do all the dishes herself. But what she did enjoy, when wearing the cook's hat, was that she was the writer, director, producer and star of her own show. The reviews weren't always spectacular but she was in control.

Mattie Lee led the rest of the family back into the kitchen. "I'm serious. What is a midge?"

Just barely able to hold onto her, and sweating profusely, Junior waddled in with Anastasia. "A tiny stinging insect that torments exposed flesh," she said. "Junior, really I'm fine. Please let me walk. But you can take my luggage up to my room."

He put her down, picked up her luggage and then headed up the back staircase, careful to step over the fourth step.

Lex grabbed his bag and followed him. "I'm just going to take my stuff upstairs, too."

Trudy Lee blew him a kiss. "Darlin', watch that fourth one."

Anastasia went over to the staircase, brought her eyes down close to examine it and then stamped her foot. "Trudy Lee Martindale, it's disgraceful the way you've neglected our ancestral mansion."

Trudy Lee completely ignored what her mother had said. "Lex, I'm sorry that you'll have to share with Roscoe, but there are fresh linens and flowers in the room." She pulled the crown roast out of the fridge and signaled to Clairese. "Come over here and hold down this piece of meat while I French bone the last chop."

Clairese slowly made her way over to the counter, sensing that maybe this wasn't such a good idea. She tentatively held onto the roast as Trudy Lee dangerously wielded the knife, scraping two inches of meat off the bone.

Mattie Lee was still confused. "A midge is an insect?"

"And she'll be buzzing in from Hollywood any minute," added Clairese.

Anastasia got to her feet and started feeling her way over to the kitchen. "What's she doing way out in California anyway?"

"She's studying to be a healer," said Clairese.

Roscoe sneaked up and gave his grandmother a kiss. "She's calling herself a channel."

"Oh, thank you, Roscoe." Anastasia looked puzzled. "A TV channel?"

He laughed. "She's coming home to cure Daddy."

Mattie Lee took a candy ball out of the jar and shoved it quickly into the side of her mouth. "She wrote to me and said she's changing her name to Florence."

Trudy Lee started to snicker. "Florence Martindale, fastest healer in the east."

They all broke out into laughter as a clanging came from the maid's room.

"What is that irritating sound?" asked Grandma Battles.

Roscoe ran out of the kitchen. "It's Dad banging in the bedroom."

Trudy Lee tied the crown roast together with kitchen string as Mattie Lee looked on.

"Can I help, Granny?"

"I told you not to call me that."

"Sorry, Trudy Lee."

Trudy Lee kissed the top of her head. "Doesn't this look yummy? This is the way my grandmother made it."

"I wish I could have known her."

Trudy Lee's face softened. "She was a Dilly."

* * * *

Of all her relatives, Trudy Lee was most like Dilly Clark King. And as often happens, Dilly was a much more compassionate and loving grandmother than a mother.

She was born in 1890, right upstairs in Trudy Lee's bedroom. The Clarks worked the land. Third generation farmers, they grew everything from corn and squash to sweet potatoes, peanuts and even soybeans.

Dilly, the prettiest daughter, was the fifth of eleven children. Just two days after her thirteenth birthday, her parents married her off to Nathaniel King, a second cousin on her father's side. The Clarks built the guest cottage out in back of Terror for the newlywed couple and without the luxury of a honeymoon, they moved in and started working on the farm immediately.

Dilly's job, above and beyond running the household and handling all the finances of the farm, was to procreate. It was demanded of her to produce her own brood and have as many babies as quickly as she could, so that there were more bodies to work the farm and do the chores. A stoic and distant mother, she ended up having ten children, the oldest one being Anastasia.

Despite her hardships, Dilly daydreamed endlessly of a life full of pomp and circumstance. A voracious reader, she would devour any book that found its way into her hands. In particular, she enjoyed tales of young heroines who transformed their existence from utter rags into abundant riches.

Of her siblings who survived, some married, some didn't, but they all moved away in hopes of better lives. All but Dilly and Nathaniel. And ultimately, they inherited Terror.

The same was true for Anastasia. The only child of Dilly's who remained in Ragland, it was very clear that after she married Papa Battles and gave birth to Trudy Lee in 1926, this would be her one and only child. So Dilly poured all of her bottled up and unused devotion upon her.

Although Dilly was an atheist, she did bow down to Mother Nature. An avid gardener, she designed and cultivated a prize winning authentic, English garden in the front quarter-acre of Terror. And she was responsible for extensive reforesting of the property after generations of relatives had profited from denuding the land of trees. In the early morning hours one could find Dilly and Trudy Lee walking arm-in-arm, taking stock of the growth progress of beech, birch, oak and pine trees that Dilly had planted with her own hands. In particular, Dilly loved the hardwoods, because they flowered and bore fruit, and were deciduous, losing their colorful leaves in winter.

Dilly wrapped her arms around the thick trunk of an old oak and smiled at Trudy Lee. "Hardwoods produce wood that is dense and heavy, making them not only structurally strong, but exceptionally beautiful as well."

"Or maybe you like hardwoods cause it's your mamma's maiden name?"

Dilly laughed deeply from her belly. "You're too smart for your britches, young lady."

But it was in the kitchen where they profoundly connected. Dilly shared her love of cooking and every recipe she could remember with her granddaughter. She was passing down their ancestral spirit through these dishes. And at night she would beg Trudy Lee to sing and dance for her. She even encouraged her dreams of becoming a bright and beautiful star on the stage, much to Anastasia's chagrin.

Trudy Lee was only twelve-years-old when Dilly died of a heart attack, at the age of forty-eight, while weeding the vegetable garden in the heat of the midday sun. And sadly, on that same day, something inside Trudy Lee was extinguished. It was a flame, a flicker that Dilly was fanning. It was a love of life and adventure that was eventually squelched by Anastasia. And although Trudy Lee had the rebelliousness to pursue a career in the arts on her own, unfortunately she didn't have the talent.

She was nowhere to be seen on the day of Dilly's funeral. Distraught over the loss of her grandmother, she chose not to share her feelings with her family for fear that they would snatch them away from her. Instead, she searched the property for the tallest tree Dilly had nurtured, and found it to be a majestic oak sitting on the back acre of the property. Trudy Lee climbed as high as possible, and when she could go no farther, she reached up into the sky in hopes of touching her grandmother one more time, and whispered, "Structurally strong, but exceptionally beautiful."

* * * *

Mattie Lee laughed. "A real Dilly dally?"

Pulled back into the present, Trudy Lee hugged her. "You bet. And it's important you learn these recipes and share them with your children too, someday. Now we spread orange zest, rosemary, garlic and olive oil all over the roast, inside and out." With her bare hands, Trudy Lee spread gobs of the paste all over the meat. "You really give it a good massage, to make sure the meat comes out tender." Like a maestro playing the piano, her hands descended upon the pork and went to town.

"It looks pretty gross," Mattie Lee giggled.

"Gross and tasty," she laughed as she dried her hands on a kitchen towel. "Now, if you'll pick up that can."

Tentatively, Mattie Lee picked up the empty soup can that was sitting on the counter.

"Wedge it into the center of the crown..."

With both hands, Mattie Lee tried to squash the can down through the center, but it wouldn't budge. She looked up at Trudy Lee who gave her a look that said *I know you can do it.* So Mattie Lee put both hands on the can, and with all her might, pushed. Suddenly, it plopped down into the center.

Trudy Lee applauded. "That will keep it from collapsing."

Roscoe came out of the maid's bedroom, sliding Bert in the rocker, as Lex headed back down into the kitchen.

"Look at that," pointed Trudy Lee. "How clever, sliding Daddy in the rocker. Lex, that must have been your idea."

"No, it was Roscoe's." He quickly went over to them. "Can I help?"

Trudy Lee put her hand up like a traffic cop. "Stop!"

Startled, Roscoe stopped with Bert in the middle of the room. She ran past them and down the front hall screaming, "Oh, my God! This is it!"

Hearing the commotion, Junior raced back down the stairs as Anastasia got to her feet. "What? Is it Bert? Is he dying? I want to see Bert before he dies." Junior swept her off her feet and ran over to Bert in the rocker with Mattie Lee and Clairese following.

Trudy Lee reentered the room. "Everyone's here." She held up a camera. "I want to capture this moment."

Lex stood there shaking his head. "Mother."

"But the Midge isn't here," Mattie Lee reminded them.

Lex touched her shoulder. "You mustn't call her that."

"Boys, stand behind your father," commanded Trudy Lee. "And Mattie Lee."

Lex, Roscoe, Mattie Lee and Junior, carrying Anastasia, stood behind Bert, who was beginning to slip out of the rocker.

Clairese joined them. "This is morbid, Trudy Lee Martindale."

"Clairese, get out of the picture. This is just for blood relatives."

Clairese stepped aside and shot her husband a look. "Junior?"

Mattie Lee began to laugh as she popped another hard candy into her mouth, and Trudy Lee motioned to Clairese. "Come over here and take this picture."

"But I'm terrible at it. I always chop the heads off."

Trudy Lee handed her the camera. "Well, you can't with this camera. It's automatic. Just push this button."

Roscoe was about to blow his top. "Let's just do it and get it over with."

Trudy Lee ran to the center of the group. She put one arm around Lex and the other touched Bert's shoulder.

Clairese peeked through the viewfinder. "Come on everyone. Smile." Trudy Lee posed like a pinup girl as Clairese repositioned herself. "Say cheese."

"No," Trudy Lee said in her Marilyn voice. "Say champagne."

Just at that moment, Mona Lee entered from the screen porch with her luggage, and the entire group shouted, "The Midge!"

She looked at them deadpan. "This space is toxic."

Clairese glanced over at Mona Lee and let the camera drop to her side as the flash went off. "Oh, now see. I've chopped your heads off."

"Welcome home, Mona Lee." Trudy Lee embraced her stiffly. "Dear, you're not wearing any make-up."

"Mother, I never wear make-up."

"Well, you should."

"I didn't come all this way for your beauty tips."

Anastasia cut in. "Hello, Mona Lee."

Mona Lee pushed Junior out of the way to see her. "Grandma Battles, what happened to your neck?"

"She had a dreadful fall," exclaimed Clairese.

Mattie Lee stepped forward, smiling, and looking at the purple turban on top of Mona Lee's head. She was thrilled to realize that they were the same height. "And we're waiting to see if she has a brain tumor."

"Concussion," corrected Junior.

Mona Lee rubbed her hands together. "I can heal you."

Lex blurted out an uncontrollable laugh. "This I've got to see."

Mona Lee walked over to him. "Oh, is that you Lex?"

"Wish him Happy Birthday," giggled Trudy Lee.

Mona Lee looked at him with disgust. "Is that why you came home? To collect your presents?"

Trudy Lee put her arm through Lex's. "That's an awful thing to say."

"Look, I don't have time to celebrate his birthday," Mona Lee said taking off her coat. "I'm here to fix Daddy. Where is he?

Where's my father?"

Trudy Lee tried to distract her. "Mona Lee, why don't you freshen up a bit and say hello to everyone, and then you can spend time with your father?"

She took a deep breath. "Mother, I can handle it. Now where is he?"

The family stepped aside, revealing Bert in the rocking chair and Mona Lee was momentarily shocked.

Trudy Lee touched her shoulder. "Dear, you must be exhausted. Why not take your things upstairs…"

"No. I have to start work now." Roscoe slid Bert into the keeping room and propped him up in the rocker. Mona Lee then made a sweeping motion with her hands. "Everybody, clear away. Now! Get away!"

Trudy Lee shook her head. "Honestly, Mona Lee."

The family fanned out as she pulled a purple velvet bag from her luggage, smiled smugly at everyone, and then knelt down and touched Bert's hand.

"Hi, Daddy. How are you feeling?"

He just stared blankly at her. *Like dancing.*

"You know I've been studying holistic medicine out on the coast, and now I can help you get better. There are plenty of things we can do. Massage? Swedish or Russian? Would you like to be Rolfed?"

Just let me rest.

"How about reflexology? That's healing by rubbing your feet? Do you want me to rub your feet?"

She dug deep into her bag. "I brought some smelly oils so we can do aromatherapy."

Lex snickered but Mona Lee stared him down.

"Or how about some guided meditation?"

She searched through her bag as Bert closed his eyes.

"It'll really relax you. We could throw the I Ching and see what the Chinese oracle suggests, or the tarot, or maybe you would like me to hypnotize you so you can go into a past life and discover what lesson you're supposed to be working out?" She finally looked up and noticed that his eyes were shut. "Daddy?" Sensing it was more serious, she called out his name more loudly. "Daddy!" Frightened, she poked him with her finger.

He suddenly snorted, opened his eyes, looked at her as though she were a stranger and then fell back to sleep again.

Holding back tears, Mona Lee got to her feet while everyone watched her.

"What the hell are you all staring at?" she cried as she ran down the hallway into the bathroom.

FIVE

BIRTHDAY PIE

Trudy Lee opened the oven door and wrestled the crown roast up onto the counter. She covered it with foil and then turned to a large bowl. "How are we for time?"

Standing next to her, Anastasia ignored her question as she fumbled to readjust her neck brace. She had changed into a different outfit, and was now wearing a bright orange pantsuit and fuchsia-colored blouse.

Trudy Lee looked over at the ingredients she had in front of her, but sensed something was off. She was making Grandma Dilly's sage and pear stuffing, and with her fingers she counted: bread cubes, broth, celery, salt, pepper, parsley and sage. "What am I missing?"

"How to cook," Anastasia whispered under her breath.

"Oh, right." Trudy Lee knocked the side of her head. "The pears." She reached for the skillet with cubed and sautéed pears and tossed the contents into the bowl with the stuffing. "Mother, how long has Mona Lee been in there with Bert?"

Anastasia looked up to the heavens. "Lifetimes."

Trudy Lee tasted the stuffing and shook her head. She banged the right cupboard facing her, which she knew would open the left one, and she took down a jar of dried sage and sprinkled some in. "I wish she would let him sleep. I want him to stay awake for the party."

Anastasia finally gave up with the neck brace. "Trudy Lee, you're not going to subject him to another family dinner?"

"I think it's important that Bert shares in celebrating Lex's birthday."

She dumped the stuffing into a casserole dish, as Anastasia made her way over to the stovetop where two large pots were boiling over. "Since when did Mona Lee start caring about Bert?"

"Since he got sick. Now she thinks he's some sort of martyr."

"Saint Bert." Anastasia brought her eyes down, very close to the kitchen counter. As she searched for a fork, the sleeve of her suit came dangerously close to the flames on the stove.

"Mother, why is she so rude to me?"

"Don't take it personally. She's a bitch to everyone." Anastasia yelped as she pricked her hand on a knife.

"She's so angry."

"Maybe she's a lesbian." Anastasia touched a spoon, and then finally found a fork, as Trudy Lee dotted the top of the stuffing with gobs of butter.

"I have given her more than any of the other kids. She always had more clothes. More toys. Her own bedroom. And now I pay her bills. How can she be so ungrateful when I give her all the things she wants?"

Anastasia raised her hand above one of the pots as her over-sized glasses steamed up. "Maybe you can't hear what she's really asking for." She harpooned a string bean, blew on it and then slipped it into her mouth.

"I mean, just look at Lex. He's the one kid who has never asked for a dime. He wouldn't even let us pay for his college tuition. And yet he gives back so much. God, I love that child."

Anastasia shook her head. "You're killing them."

"I beg your pardon?"

"The vegetables." She spat the green bean out into her hand. "You overcook the vegetables and they taste like mush."

Trudy Lee untied her apron and threw it onto the floor. "Well, then you do it!"

"Don't get mad. You're so over-sensitive."

Having had enough, Trudy Lee took a deep breath and slowly turned to her. "Say it. I know you're thinking it."

"What?"

"I'm a rotten cook."

She shrugged her shoulders. "You're not a rotten cook. You just overdo everything."

Anastasia bent down and picked up the apron, stepping right into the pie mixture still on the floor. For a moment she couldn't move her foot. "What's this crap on the floor?"

"Oh, and now I suppose you're going to tell me I keep a terrible house?"

"Well?" she said trying to pull her foot free.

"I give up!"

"Trudy Lee, why do you do this? Every time the family gets together you make things so complicated. You set yourself up for disaster, and when it happens you just play it to the hilt. Why don't you just calm down and...?"

"Why are you here?"

"Oh God." Anastasia slipped her shoe off and sniffed the bottom of it.

Trudy Lee raised her voice and turned her head to the maid's room. "It's not because of Bert, because I know you can't stand him. You never could."

"That's a lie," Anastasia said in a hushed whisper as she wiped her shoe on the apron. "Bert's a good man."

"Then are you here to humiliate me in front of my husband and kids? Because if you are, you're doing a great job of it. Always making fun of me. Criticizing my make-up. My cooking. My house. My life. You make me feel three-feet-tall."

Anastasia tried to get out of it with humor. "No, Mona Lee is three-feet-tall."

"You're so perfect, why don't you take over? They'd love it. They all adore you!"

Trudy Lee ran up the back staircase as Mattie Lee skipped in through the screen porch.

Anastasia hollered up after her daughter. "If you want sympathy you'll find it in the dictionary between shit and syphilis."

Mattie Lee slipped a hard candy from one cheek to the other. "Between shit and what?"

"Mattie Lee?" Anastasia asked as she slipped on her shoe. "Will you help me into the front salon?"

"Sure Grandma Battles."

Together they walked down the hallway, creaking floorboards as they made their way to the front of Terror. "Have you ever gone down into the basement and looked up at the ceiling?"

Mattie Lee was at a loss. "What?"

"The creaking of the floorboards. What does that sound remind you of?"

Her great granddaughter thought hard as they passed rows of family pictures hanging on the walls. "Maybe a…ship?"

Anastasia squeezed Mattie Lee's arm gently into her side, acknowledging how smart she was. "Next time you're down there, look up. You'll see some boards are painted different colors, others are worn deep with grooves. But they all come from the same source. Your great, great, great, great, grandfather." She paused for a moment, counting her fingers. "Was that enough greats?" Mattie Lee giggled. "Well, your relative, Thaddeus Clark was a sea captain. And when he bought this property he dismantled his beloved ship, the Rebecca Stern, which was named after his mother, and he used its timber to build this house."

"Wow," Mattie Lee gasped. "All those memories built right into Terror."

"Frightening thought, isn't it?"

Mattie Lee shivered as she squeezed Anastasia's arm. "It's kinda damp in here tonight."

"Colder than a witch's tit." Anastasia grabbed her neck as Mattie Lee smiled. "And this damn brace is giving me a headache." She ripped it off.

Upstairs, having no idea where she was running to, Trudy Lee collapsed into one of the two chairs flanking the mahogany lowboy at the top of the landing. Tired and frustrated, she really wanted to have a good cry, but the moment she allowed herself the luxury of the indulgence, she dried up.

She leaned against the piece of furniture and unconsciously touched the curve of the cabriole leg. Her hand slid across the top of the chest and underneath the intricate runner Anastasia had crocheted decades ago. But the moment her index finger dipped into one of the rough grooves, she snapped out of her stupor. Without looking, she felt for the other gashes and then bit her lower lip.

She tried as hard as she could to remember why she had taken a hot poker stick to the only family heirloom her father had managed to bring over from Scotland, but, for the life of her, she couldn't. She did recall that she couldn't have been older than Mattie Lee at the time and that she had had a fight with Anastasia. But what the rage was all about completely escaped her. As angry as she was with her mother, Trudy Lee was grateful that Anastasia had never told Papa Battles what she had done, for both mother and daughter were certain he would have taken the same poker stick to Trudy Lee.

She heard laughter wafting up the front stairs and got up from her chair. She stood in the doorway of the back bedroom and noticed Lex's bag on the bed. Zipped open, she was drawn to it. On top was his sweater, which she slowly brought up to her face. She breathed in as deeply as possible and smiled. She looked down and noticed a bottle of pills. She picked them up but without her glasses she struggled to make out what they were.

"Mother?" Lex asked, standing in the doorway with a black shoebox in his hands.

She spun around, dropping the pills into the bag.

"Dear."

"What are you doing?"

"I…um…I'm just so happy you're here." She rushed over and touched his arm. "Oh, I almost forgot. I made your favorite taste treat."

"My favorite what?" he asked cautiously.

"Devils on horseback."

He honestly had never heard of these before in his life. "What?"

"I stuffed pitted dates with herbed goat cheese instead of chicken livers, and wrapped them in bacon. They're all made up in the fridge. I just have to pop them under the broiler."

He laughed. "Devils?"

"Or I could make it angels and substitute the dates with apricots."

"No, no, devils are fine."

Back on track and on a mission, Trudy Lee rushed out of the room and down the hallway. "Great. They'll be ready in just a few."

She flew down the back staircase as Lex shook his head. Wondering if she had deciphered the prescription on the bottle, he zipped up his bag, put it into the closet and left the room.

Mattie Lee was stoking the fire in the front salon when suddenly a log rolled off the grate, snapping sparks left and right. One flew up over the fireplace screen and landed on the edge of the Persian rug.

Mattie Lee jumped back. "Syphilis."

Anastasia looked over at her. "What dear?"

As quickly as it started to smoke, Mattie Lee's shoe was on top of it, while Lex came down the front staircase with the shoebox.

"Watcha got there, Uncle Lex?"

"A whole bunch of pictures," he said as he entered the salon. "Who's that?" he asked pointing to a watercolor portrait hanging over the mantel.

"I don't know," Mattie Lee said as she squinted at it. "It's all out of focus."

"You losing your eyes too, dear?" Anastasia asked, having almost fallen asleep.

She squinted harder. "No, Grandma Battles. It's really out of focus."

"Come over here, Mattie Lee," Lex said as he sat down on the rug with the box. He took a picture out and handed it to her. "Look. Here's a photo of Bert on a diving board."

Mattie Lee picked it up and a huge smile appeared on her face. "I didn't know he could swim."

"Oh sure. He was a competitive diver in college."

"Did you know that, Grandma Battles?" she asked.

Anastasia let out a gentle snore.

Mattie Lee looked more closely at the picture. "He was so handsome."

"It's kind of hard seeing Grandpa Bert like this, isn't it?"

She put his picture back into the box gently. "Yeah, but I don't want him to suffer anymore."

In Bert's room, Mona Lee was finishing up her last treatment. She was sitting on the edge of his bed and had his pajama top pushed up so his belly was exposed. She held a large paper funnel pointing down at his navel. Incense and candles were burning as Mona Lee brought her lips to the large end of the cone.

"Daddy? Cancer is the physical manifestation of anger and resentment. Your demons are safe with me. You can confide in me. You can share with me. You can talk to me. Talk to me." She started to shout into the funnel. "Talk to me. Oh, demons that have a stranglehold on my daddy, let go of his liver. Let go of his kidneys. Let go of his lungs and heart and be off with you." Her body then started to swing like a pendulum faster and faster as she moaned. "Oooooohhh! Oooooohhh! Oooooohhh!"

She stopped moving and put her face into the funnel. At the top of her lungs she shouted, "Aahhheeeeeooooowwww!"

Awakened from his semi-conscious sleep, Bert bolted upright. Frightened, Mona Lee dropped the cone and fell off the bed.

"Who's that shouting?" asked Grandma Battles, waking up from her snooze in the front salon.

Trudy Lee appeared in the entrance to the parlor, holding the tray of devils on horseback, waiting for someone to notice her.

Mona Lee came running down the hallway, rubbing her hands together. "I think I shrunk one of his tumors. So, who's next? Grandma Battles?"

"Hurt me and you're out the door."

Trudy Lee cleared her throat and entered the room. "Devils on horseback?"

Mona Lee stood behind the divan. "Now Grandma, just relax. I'm going to give you a little shiatsu." She shoved her hands under Anastasia's neck, causing her head to pop forward.

"I don't want anything that sounds like a dog."

"That's Shih Tzu," Mattie Lee said correcting her.

"Child, watch your mouth," Trudy Lee scolded as she walked over to Lex. "Your devil on horseback, sir."

He picked one off the tray and popped it into his mouth. The salty, sweet, smoky combination was sublime and his face lit up. "Mother, these are wonderful."

Trudy Lee smiled knowingly as she put the tray down on the coffee table and straightened the painting. "Lex darling?" She posed dramatically underneath it. "Did you see whose portrait is above the mantel?"

"Mother, I have no idea who that is."

"Look harder," she said.

Mona Lee squinted. "It's so blurry."

"Vladimir did it in the impression style," Trudy Lee announced proudly.

"Yeah, bad impression," laughed Anastasia.

"Vladimir the cab driver?" Lex asked. "I didn't know he could paint."

"He can't," laughed Mona Lee.

Trudy Lee put her hands on her hips. "Impressionism is like 3-D. You all have to cross your eyes a bit and you'll see who it is."

All of them sat there, staring at the painting with their eyes crossed. No one said a word.

"Well, it doesn't take a rocket scientist." Annoyed, Trudy Lee gestured to the portrait. "Look at it. She has blonde hair and a pink dress, and although he added a few extra pounds, I think Vladimir painted a masterpiece. Can't anyone guess who it is?"

There was a long pause.

Mattie Lee innocently piped up. "Miss Piggy?"

"Honestly." Exasperated, Trudy Lee grabbed a devil on horse-back and threw it into her mouth.

"Ah," sighed Mona Lee, "the Martindale women learn so young."

"You ninnies, it's me." Trudy Lee touched the frame lovingly. "You're all so cynical." They ignored her as she walked about the room, straightening knickknacks, hungry for attention.

Mona Lee stuck her hands behind Anastasia's neck and started massaging it roughly.

"Just relax, Grandma Battles. That's it. Oh, so tight. They say neck tension represents bullheadedness."

"You're pushing it Mona Lee."

"Exactly. Shiatsu is finger pressure. Oohhh, feel this big old knot? Now Grandma, picture this gnarled muscle as a giant slab of butter, melting on a red-hot baked potato. Just feel it melting and oozing down into that fluffy white spud. Oohh, yeah, melt that knot of butter. There. Now, how do you feel, Grandma Battles?"

"Hungry, let's eat."

Trudy Lee hesitated and then made an attempt at connecting with Mona Lee. "Dear, you have a real flair for that shizado."

"Yes, I know and it's shiatsu." She took a bundle of sage and matches out of her purple velvet satchel.

"Do you have a lot of clients?" Lex asked.

Mona Lee struck a match with aggressiveness. "What's that supposed to mean?"

Lex looked at her as if she were an idiot. "It's supposed to mean, do you have a lot of clients?"

"Well, none that have returned." Everyone in the room looked at each other. "But my master says it takes time to build up a clientele list. Meanwhile, I'm learning acupuncture."

Dumbfounded and apprehensive, everyone just watched her as she lit the sage on fire, walked around the salon and then down the hallway.

"What the hell is she doing?" whispered Trudy Lee.

Anastasia smiled. "Mmmmm, I smell pot."

"Mother!"

"Grandma Battles, how do you know what marijuana smells like?" asked Lex.

"Me and the girls up in Detroit just love it. The doctor gives it to us for our eyes."

Trudy Lee walked into the foyer as Roscoe hip-checked the front door open and slowly closed it, not knowing she was standing there.

"Roscoe?" He jumped when he heard her voice. "Did Junior pick up my van?"

"Yeah, I drove back his car."

She gave him a look of disapproval as he followed her down the hallway to the kitchen.

"All I asked you to do was watch Lex's pie."

"I..."

"I barely had time to make another one. Why would you want to sabotage his birthday?"

As Trudy Lee entered the kitchen, Roscoe punched the hallway wall. A framed picture fell and he caught it, just as Trudy Lee glanced back at him. She gave him another look of disdain.

In the kitchen she whipped the foil off the roast, and started putting white paper caps on the end of each bone. Roscoe appeared as Mona Lee zipped by with the sage burning and flew into Bert's room.

Trudy Lee squinted at the thermometer stuck in the roast. "What temperature does pork have to come up to? One-twenty should be fine. Look Roscoe, I wrote each person's name on a frilly cap so they know which chop is theirs."

Nonplussed, he just looked at it. Mona Lee came out of the maid's room where they could hear Bert coughing, as Trudy Lee put her hand up to her nose. "Oh, Mona Lee, that stuff smells just awful. It'll ruin Lex's birthday dinner."

"It's not stuff, Mother. It's sage and it's cleansing the air of negative energy."

"Well then, breathe deep, dear."

Both Trudy Lee and Roscoe coughed as Mona Lee circled the kitchen, hopped over the fourth step and ran upstairs with the burning sage.

Struggling to clear her throat, Trudy Lee shouted down the hallway. "Everybody, dinner's almost ready." She turned around and saw Roscoe eyeing the bourbon bottle. "Roscoe? Can you finish setting the dining room table?"

Reluctantly, he opened a bottom cupboard and reached up and pushed out a drawer. He gave Trudy Lee a dirty look behind her back and grabbed a handful of over-worn silverware, and walked down the hallway to the dining room.

In the salon, Anastasia had closed her eyes again as Lex and Mattie Lee looked at more pictures.

"How did you do this, Uncle Lex?"

He held up a black and white picture. "I re-photographed all these old, torn pictures, and see, they come out looking brand new."

"Who's that?"

"That's me when I was six months old."

Mattie Lee looked harder. "Who's the man holding you?"

Lex laughed and elbowed her. "That's not a man. That's Aunt Butch."

"What's wrong with your leg?"

"I was born with a club foot and they put it in a cast to bend it…" Lex paused and moved the photo back and forth. "They put it in a cast to bend it back into…" He covered his left eye with his hand and then took it away. He covered it again. "Oh no."

"What's wrong, Uncle Lex?"

He looked across the room and focused on the portrait and saw a zigzag flashing light. Panicking, he looked up at Grandma Battles and tried to bring her into focus. "Damn it, I'm having an aura."

"A what?"

"Oh, Mattie Lee. It's my warning that a migraine is coming. I can't see out of my left eye and now the left side of my face is going numb."

"Do you want a cold face cloth?"

He put both hands to his head. "Oh God, I don't think I brought my Midrin."

"Do you want an aspirin?"

He broke out into a flop sweat as he rubbed his left arm. "No thanks honey. It wouldn't do any good."

"I'm sorry."

Lex looked back over at Grandma Battles, whose eyes were still closed, and whispered to Mattie Lee, "We can't let Trudy know this is happening. It'll spoil everything."

"It'll be our secret."

Clairese and Junior entered through the squeaky screen porch door, carrying a huge casserole dish and a large bottle of wine.

"Gotcha your white wine, Mother," Junior shouted proudly, as

Mona Lee came back downstairs.

Trudy Lee looked at the bottle. "I asked for red. You all know white wine doesn't go with crown roast."

Clairese shook her head. "But it's the other white meat."

Mona Lee lifted the foil that was covering the roast and crinkled her nose. "Tell me you're not serving pork."

Feeling attacked, Trudy Lee spun around towards her, wielding the carving knife. "Well, what the hell do you think I've been slaving over while you've been playing witch doctor?"

Frightened, Mona Lee actually backed off, while in the salon Mattie Lee and Lex each slid an arm under an armpit of Grandma Battles and brought her to a standing position. "What?" she murmured. "Is it Bert? Is he going?"

"No," giggled Mattie Lee. "We're going to eat."

Across the main foyer and in the dining room, Roscoe had opened the bottle of wine, poured himself a glass and chugged half of it down. He refilled it, and then began to fill everyone else's glass but Mattie Lee's.

The large table was covered with a faded and stained white tablecloth, crocheted decades ago by Bert's great grandmother. It was elegantly set with mismatched china and glassware, while two large silver candelabra, holding five white candles each, anchored the far ends.

"Mona Lee can have vegetables," Lex suggested as Trudy Lee entered and put her oversized serving dish onto the table.

She looked at Clairese and Junior as they appeared in the doorway. "Did you bring the scalloped potatoes?"

They just looked at each other again.

"What?" screamed Trudy Lee. "You forgot them? You forgot Lex's favorite?"

"I thought you were doing the scalloped potatoes," Clairese said as Junior put the dish on the table. "I did carrots and turnips."

Simultaneously, Trudy Lee and Clairese opened their lids as if it were a competition.

"No, I did carrots and turnips. Now the whole dinner's ruined," Trudy Lee cried, as she threw up her hands. She ran into the kitchen and had a meltdown. They could hear her cursing left and right as she banged and slammed anything that wasn't bolted down.

"Mother, it's not ruined," Lex shouted as he rubbed the back of his neck. "I love carrots and turnips."

Mona Lee flicked her fingers at the dish. "Root vegetables should be eaten in the fall, not spring."

Then, as if nothing had happened, Trudy Lee came back, calm and collected, carrying the roast. "Roscoe, get your father."

Roscoe ran down to Bert's room as Trudy Lee gestured to the table. "Everybody sit, dinner's going to get cold."

She scooted back into the kitchen as the family tentatively sat down at the table. As she came back in juggling the rolls, the stuffing and the string beans, an out of breath Roscoe reappeared. "Pop's asleep."

"Damn it," Trudy Lee swore. "I knew this would happen." She looked at all of them. "No, no. You're sitting all wrong. I want Grandma Battles to my left, then Roscoe." Reluctantly, but unsurprised, they all got up and changed seats. "Then Junior, Mona Lee, Mattie Lee, Clairese and then Lex to my right."

Trudy Lee sat down and then suddenly jumped to her feet and ran down the hallway.

"Where did she go?" asked Junior.

"Let's eat," Anastasia said as she picked up her fork. "I'm starving."

Everyone started dishing out food as Trudy Lee came back to the table with her camera. "Stop! Put that food back. Put it all back. Real nice like."

The family members scraped the food off of their plates, and ridiculously, tried to get it back onto the respective serving dishes, to make it look as though nothing had been disturbed.

"Ready, say champagne," Trudy Lee ordered with a breathy voice. The camera flashed as she took the picture and Lex put his hands up to his eyes. "Now we can start. Your names are on your chops." All but Trudy Lee filled their plates as Junior sliced each chop off the roast. "Aw, see, Bert should be here carving. You're butchering it, Junior."

Once he could see again, Lex looked down at her plate. "Mother, aren't you going to eat?"

"No, I'm on a diet."

"Yeah," snickered Anastasia. "A leftover diet. She eats everything that's left over."

Everyone laughed but Trudy Lee.

"Very funny, Mother."

Junior started to eat, but Clairese grabbed his arm. "Stop Junior. We have to say grace first."

"Jesus Christ," shouted Mona Lee.

"Amen!" declared everyone but Clairese as they started to eat.

"It's the devil!" Clairese said looking up to the Lord. "They're all full of the devil."

Junior lifted his fork. "The carrots and turnips are great, Mother."

Blowing it off, Trudy Lee shrugged her shoulders. "Clairese's are probably better."

"Mmmmm," said Clairese. "The stuffing is wonderful."

Trudy Lee shook her head. "It came out a little dry."

"Will you stop Mother," Lex demanded. "Can't you take a compliment?"

Roscoe examined his piece of meat. "The crown roast is…"

Trudy Lee cut him off before he could criticize it. "Overdone."

"No. I think there's writing on my chop," he said with disbelief.

Trudy Lee leaned across the table and strained to see his plate. "What?"

Clairese picked up her dish and examined it closely. "Mine says…chicken noodle."

Trudy Lee's jaw dropped. "Oh, no. Mattie Lee forgot to take the label off the soup can."

Mattie Lee looked over at her, shocked as Lex tried to smooth things over. "We can pick it away."

Mona Lee pushed her plate away. "Eat that meat and you'll need a high colonic."

"I'll have a gin and tonic," shouted Anastasia.

"Mona Lee?" Trudy Lee looked over at her full glass. "You aren't having any wine?"

She shook her head emphatically. "I gave up alcohol. My astrologer says I have five houses in water, and I shouldn't drink because I'll attract depressed souls."

"Dead or alive?" asked Anastasia.

Everyone but Mona Lee laughed.

Trudy Lee pointed at Lex's plate. "Darling, you haven't touched a thing."

Anastasia reached across the table. "Is that butter?" The cuff of her blouse caught on Trudy Lee's wine glass, knocking it over.

Lex pushed himself away from the table to escape getting wet, while Trudy Lee reached for her napkin.

"Mother, you knocked my wine over into Lex's plate. Now, he'll have to start all over."

"It's all right," he said getting up from the table. "I'll get another plate."

He took his plate into the kitchen and rested his head against the refrigerator, wondering how much more of this he could take.

Trudy Lee sighed. "I just wanted everything to be just so for Lex's twenty-ninth birthday."

Mona Lee choked.

"Mother," Roscoe said. "Lex is five years older than me and I'm thirty-one."

Trudy Lee did a double take. "What?"

"He is, Mother," Junior agreed. "I'm thirty-eight."

"And I'm freaking forty," moaned Mona Lee.

ARTHUR WOOTEN

"Stop, you're all being silly," Trudy Lee said, laughing at all of them.

Lex returned to the table with a clean plate. "No, Mother. I am thirty-six."

"But that's impossible." She looked at them, desperately. "Because I was born the same year, the same month..."

They all recited with her, "...The same day, the same hour as Marilyn Monroe."

"And the day she died," Trudy Lee gasped, "I was deathly sick."

They all continued to eat.

Trudy Lee looked at Lex and he nodded. She put her hands to her chest and started to breathe deeply. In a little girl's voice she asked, "So, how old am I?"

"Mother," Mona Lee said exasperated. "You are so pathetic. Of all people to emulate."

Anastasia chimed in. "Yes, why didn't you pick someone classy, like Katherine Hepburn?"

"Or powerful, like Indira Ghandi?" suggested Mona Lee.

Clairese raised her hand. "Or a good Christian, like Ann B. Davis?"

They all turned to her, having no idea whom she was talking about.

"Alice on The Brady Bunch? She gave all her money to God."

Not surprised at the stupid suggestion, and no one even wanting to challenge her on this one, they all ignored her.

"Because," Trudy Lee reminded them, "Marilyn is a legend."

"She was a mess," declared Mona Lee.

Clairese looked up to the Lord. "And she lived a life of sin."

Anastasia held up her glass. "And then she was murdered."

Trudy Lee came to her defense. "Marilyn is beautiful."

"Was beautiful," snorted Mona Lee. "Imagine what she'd look like today?"

Trudy Lee dropped her head. "But everyone loved her." She

80

got up from the table and ran into the kitchen.

Chalking it up to another Martindale dinner, Anastasia, Junior, Clairese and Mattie Lee continued to eat dinner ravenously.

"What's her problem?" asked Mona Lee.

"You," shouted Roscoe.

She watched him as he finished another glass of wine. "Oh that's right. Blame it on me."

"You come in here all high and mighty, like you're the queen or something, and then you put down and make fun of everything she does or says."

Mona Lee gestured to the whole table. "You do it. You all do it."

Roscoe continued. "And then you show up with this asinine idea that you're going to heal Pop."

"Well, it's a lot more than any of you are doing. Just laughing and joking and celebrating Lex's birthday."

"Mona Lee face it, Dad is dying. And yes, we are laughing and celebrating 'cause that's the way he wants it."

She intentionally responded in such a low whisper that everyone had to strain to hear her. "No, Roscoe, it's the way Mother wants it."

Once he was able to decipher her statement, he blew his top. "It's so easy for you, Mona Lee. Flying in and out, always on the outside. Never committing to anything."

Mona Lee nodded her head to everyone else at the table. "Oh, listen everyone. Mr. No Job says I never commit."

"At least I've had jobs. You've never worked a day in your life."

She took great delight in what she was about to say. "Oh, do you mean the million-dollar-a-year bartending job in Alaska, or the million-dollar-a-year job working the state fair circuit, running the tilt-a-whirl?"

Roscoe slammed his fist on the table. "I have the most important job of my life right now. Day and night I take care of Dad. I read to him. I carry him to the bathroom. I wash the urine and feces off him. That's a lot more than what you're doing. Running around the house burning weeds. And don't think we all don't know that you took their vacation money."

She was truly thrown. "What vacation money?"

Roscoe knew he was onto something that would get under her skin. "The money Mother scraped together so she and Dad could go away before he got too sick. But now it's too late. You had to cry Mommy. The only time you're ever nice to her is when you need money. And in her desperate attempt to make you love her, like a fool, she gives it to you."

Again Mona Lee brought her voice down to a whisper. "How sad. A thirty-one-year-old son who lives with his parents and speaks in superlatives. And aren't you the brother with the drinking problem? Is that booze I see in your glass? Mamma's little boy is off the wagon again. You're right, I'm wrong. Mother isn't the pathetic one, you are."

Roscoe leaned across the table towards her. "You're just jealous!"

"Of you, Roscoe? Ha!"

His lips curled into an evil smile. "No, of Mother. You're jealous because she's pretty and you're not."

"You're sicker than I thought."

He waved at her diminutive stature. "She has more style in her little finger than you have in your entire body."

Mona Lee had to pull out the stops. "It's all clear to me now. In twenty years you'll still be living with Mother, obeying her every command, just begging for her approval and she'll still be loving Lex."

"You God damn…" Roscoe leaped towards Mona Lee and Junior caught him.

In a flash, Mona Lee got up from the table and ran upstairs.

"…Bitch!" Frustrated, Roscoe looked at everyone at the table and then ran out the front door of Terror.

There was a moment of silence.

"Could someone please pass the butter?" Anastasia asked, as though nothing had happened.

Mattie Lee passed it to her as Lex dropped his head into his hands.

Suddenly the lights went out, and Trudy Lee walked into the dining room, carrying the birthday pie with thirty-six candles burning.

"Happy Birthday to you...Come on everybody," encouraged Trudy Lee.

They all sang. "Happy Birthday to you. Happy Birthday dear Lex, Happy Birthday to you."

Trudy Lee placed the pie in front of him as he tried not to look at the candles.

She touched his shoulder. "You have to make a wish, Lex."

The candles were blazing in front of him.

"Ready?" asked Trudy Lee.

In unison, everyone shouted, "One, two, three!"

There was a heaving sound and the candles went out.

The room went pitch black. Just before everyone could cheer, Bert appeared at the dining room door. He was lit from behind and only his frightening silhouette could be seen.

"Aaaahhhhh!" screamed Clairese.

"Junior, get the lights," ordered Trudy Lee.

Junior turned the lights back on as she ran over and supported Bert. "What happened?" she asked looking around the dining room. "Where did Lex go?"

Mattie Lee looked at the table. "He threw up on the pie."

SIX

THE IMMACULATE DECEPTION

Clairese held onto the car door with all her might. "Junior, I'm not letting you go till you tell me what's wrong."

"I have a doctor's appointment," he shouted from inside the car.

Mattie Lee watched from behind the big magnolia bush that sat between Terror and the Slaves' Quarters.

"But you just went yesterday. And what kind of doctor sees patients on a Friday evening?"

"A professional one. Now step away from the car, Clairese. I'll be home by nine."

She held onto the car as if she could keep it from speeding off. "We have to talk about this Junior. We talk about everything."

"You talk about everything," he whispered under his breath, as he inched the car away from her. She finally let go and he zoomed down the driveway.

"One, two, three, four, five, six, seven, eight," he counted as the trees beat their fists against his car.

"What is going on around here?" Clairese asked herself. Not wearing a coat, she shivered as she ran over to Terror's screen

84

porch. "Mattie Lee? Mattie Lee Martindale, are you in there?"

Trudy Lee opened the kitchen window. "No she's not, Clairese, and stop your yelling. Bert just fell back to sleep." She slammed the window shut.

"Mattie Lee?" Clairese called out. "I know you're up in one of these trees." She ran to the base of an old spruce. "I'm warning you." She checked another tree. "Get into the house this instant." She ran back to the open door of the Slaves' Quarters. "You've got some piano playing to do, young lady!" She waited a moment and then slammed the door shut.

Mattie Lee emerged from the magnolia bush and ran down the hill behind the house to the abandoned chicken coop that sat on the edge of the Lovejoy's property. She darted inside and closed the door.

She fumbled for a pack of matches lying on a small wooden crate, and lit a candle. This was Mattie Lee's place, her sanctuary from her parents. Her family. It was her place to dream. On each side of the shed were rows of wide shelving where the chickens had made their roosts. She had cleaned most of it out; however, there were still the remains of some feathers and hay.

She pulled a handful of hard candies out of her pocket and put them into an empty coffee can. She also took out a wrinkled picture, torn from a magazine. She grabbed a rock and tacked the picture up onto the wooden wall with a rusty nail, alongside dozens of other pictures, all of horribly disfigured people. Pictures of burn victims, car crashes and birth defects. Some showed the ravages of facial cancer, flesh eating diseases, and amputations.

Mattie Lee stood back and looked at them lovingly. And then she started to cry. Softly at first, and then she really started to bawl.

She heard a twig snap suddenly outside the coop and she blew the candle out.

"Hel-lo? Is somebody in there?" the voice called out.

Mattie Lee wiped her tears and scrunched her face trying to

figure out who it was.

"Hello?" the voice asked again.

She quietly stuck her head out of the pane less window.

"Lowell? Lowell Lovejoy?" she whispered. "Is that you?"

"Mattie Lee?"

She ran over and opened the door. "Get in here."

Lowell hesitated. He was seven and very small for his age. A product of Delbert and Betsy Metal, Lowell had ten fingers and ten toes, but not all of his brains.

She grabbed his arm. "Come on, hurry up!"

She pulled him in quickly, looked around outside, and then closed the door.

He stood motionless as she lit the candle again. Betsy may have called him cute but the truth was he was downright goofy looking. He had a buzzed haircut and ears that stuck straight out. He wore brown horn-rimmed glasses, and already had a mouthful of crooked teeth.

"Hey, Mattie Lee. I was in my backyard counting the needles on one of our pine trees when it got dark and I lost count and had to start over and then I thought I heard someone crying."

"Crying?" she asked pretending to be confused.

"Yeah."

"Oh that? I was acting. Like in a play."

"Boy you're really good." His eyes started to adjust to the light. "What is this place?"

She looked at it with pride. "My secret hideout."

"Gosh, I've never been in a secret hideout before."

"Well then, rule number one: anything we talk about in here is secret. Got it?"

"Got it."

He focused on the pictures nailed to the walls. "Oh gawd! These are awful. Why do you have all these terrible pictures up, Mattie Lee?"

"They aren't terrible, Lowell. They are victims. Victims of fate.

You have to respect them."

"I respect them. But do we have to look at them? Gawd. That one's missing the whole side of a face!"

"It's hard to look at, but we must. I'm going to be a doctor. And someday I'm going to reconstruct somebody's face or reattach an arm and stuff like that."

"My daddy sent my mother to a doctor for reconstruction."

"Why?"

"Cause he said her boobs were too droopy. So they put in fake ones and they hardened all up and she can't lie on her stomach cause of the constant pain, and she won't let my daddy touch them now."

"Serves him right. My Uncle Lex says your daddy is a Mormon." Mattie Lee gazed at the pictures. "Someday I'm going to be a doctor and help people with real problems."

Lowell looked closely at the pictures. "I think I'm going to be sick. And what's that smell?"

"Just breathe through your mouth. Chicken shit."

"I'm not a chicken shit!"

"No, Lowell, the smell is chicken shit. This used to be a coop."

His nose started to twitch and then he sneezed. "My allergies. You had chickens?"

"My Uncle Roscoe did. My daddy joined in, thinking he could leave his accounting job. They tried to make millions of dollars but the plan laid an egg."

"And now your daddy hates your mamma cause she's a deranged religious woman."

"That's not true, Lowell Lovejoy. That's absolutely not true. Who's spreading that vicious lie around school?"

"You are."

"Oh." She dashed to the window and looked out into the dark night. "Well, since we are in my secret hideout and you've promised not to tell, it is true." She turned back to Lowell. "My daddy says my mother is high strung."

"My mother's high strung. She's going to have another baby."

"Another? That makes twelve kids, Lowell!"

"I know. My daddy laughed, saying, 'cheaper by the dozen.'"

"And your mother?"

"She cried. But she said I'm her favorite."

Mattie Lee moved over next to him. "Why's that?"

"Cause I was the easiest birth, so far. She was standing in line at the bank and out I came. No warning. No pain. I guess after having the nine before me, I just kinda walked out. She said it's the easiest deposit she ever made."

"Amazing." Mattie Lee looked at him seriously. "Lowell, how long have I known you?"

"All my life."

"Is that long enough to ask you a personal question?"

He pondered hard. "I think so."

"And remember, this is a secret, so you can't tell anyone I asked."

"OK."

Mattie Lee hesitated and then just blurted out the question. "How do you think a girl gets pregnant?"

Lowell bit his lower lip. "Didn't you ask your mother?"

"Yes. She said, 'you don't!' But I overheard Becky Sue Potter explaining it to some of the other girls at school lunch. But it got confusing."

"How so, Mattie Lee?"

"First you have an egg."

"I heard that too. But what kind of egg?"

Mattie Lee thought hard. "I don't know. Sunnyside up? OK, so you have an egg on an Ethiopian tube."

Lowell scratched his head. "What's an Ethiopian tube?"

"I'm not sure. Maybe a breakfast roll?"

"Does it have to be breakfast, 'cause I like eggs for dinner?"

"No, Lowell. It can only happen when Venus enters Virginia."

They both looked at each other.

"Venus?" he asked.

Frustrated, Mattie Lee threw her arms up. "You know your planets don't you?"

"Yes, Mattie Lee, but how can Venus enter Virginia?"

She walked over to the window and looked up at the night sky. "I think it means that when the planet Venus comes into view over the state of Virginia, and you have an egg on an Ethiopian tube, you'll get pregnant."

Lowell took in what she had said, but then disagreed. "No, you've got it all wrong. I heard my daddy telling my older brothers. He said, 'if a woman has an egg and the man has…'" He forgot the rest.

Mattie Lee put her hands on her hips. "And the man has what, smarty pants?"

"If a woman has an egg and the man has the…germs! And they get together, pow! She'll get pregnant."

Mattie Lee was quiet a moment and then confessed, "Well, I knew that all along. I was just testing you."

Lowell and Mattie Lee found themselves standing very close to one another and laughed nervously. The laughter stopped and there was an awkward moment. Lowell inched a bit closer to her and she backed up, bumping into the old chicken roost. He got up on his tiptoes as she sat down on the roost, and they awkwardly tried to find the right positions for their noses.

They kissed quickly and very innocently. They pulled away, and unexpectedly, Lowell sneezed all over Mattie Lee. She brought her hands up to her face and realized she was holding onto an old chicken's egg.

They looked at each other and then put two and two together. Panicked, Lowell ran out of the shed crying, "Aaaaahhh!"

"Oh no! Oh no!" Mattie Lee dropped the egg, blew out the candle and ran back up the hill to the Slaves' Quarters holding her stomach. "Jesus fucking Christ!"

As Mattie Lee ran past Terror, crying, the light in the back upstairs bedroom went out. Mona Lee came down the staircase as Trudy Lee finished up washing the dishes.

"Did your herbal remedy help Lex?"

"He threw it up," Mona Lee said, while washing her hands. "He's back in bed and trying to sleep it off."

"Poor kid," Trudy Lee said while handing her a dish to dry. "I know his migraines are because of a defective gene he inherited from me."

Mona Lee ignored the plate and pulled out the blender. "You don't get headaches, Mother." She peeled a banana and threw it into the blender.

Trudy Lee dried the dish, dramatically. "No but I get the aura. I lose my vision and my hands go numb."

"Then it goes away." Mona Lee grabbed a handful of strawberries and some ice from the fridge and threw it into the blender.

"I knew you didn't eat enough at dinner, Mona Lee. Being vegetarian is very tricky. You need a nutritionist to help make sure you're getting enough protein."

"I know what I'm doing." She opened a protein packet and dumped it into the mixture. "Where do you keep the vodka now?"

Trudy Lee looked at her sarcastically. "But I thought you attracted depressed souls?"

"Fuck the souls. I need a drink."

"The cabinet next to the bread drawer. But don't tell Roscoe."

Mona Lee grabbed the vodka and poured freely into the blender. She churned it all up, poured it out into a large glass and started gulping it down.

Trudy Lee tried not to react. "Anyway, until my aura goes away, I just know I'm going to die. It's awful Mona Lee."

"Whatever," she mumbled as she guzzled.

She put both hands to her heart. "And it just hurts me so, seeing my Lex in such agony."

"Everything is Lex! Lex! Lex!" Mona Lee picked up the blender to pour the rest into her glass, when the bottom dropped out, spilling the drink onto the floor. Surprisingly, she started to cry.

"Mona Lee, are those tears?"

She quickly turned her back to her. "Yes, Mother. I do cry."

Trudy Lee was sincerely shocked. "Incredible."

"Stop it! You make me sound like some kind of monster." She cried harder.

"Well, every time I try to get close to you, you push me away." Trudy Lee tried to embrace her.

"I don't want you close to me," she said pushing her away. "I just don't want it to be all about Lex. I have problems too."

"OK." Trudy Lee stood there in silence as Mona Lee put her fist to her forehead. "Do you want to talk about it?"

"Cold drink headache," she screamed.

Trudy Lee grabbed a roll of paper towels. "Well, if that's your problem."

"Mother?"

"Yes?"

Mona Lee took a large gulp of the drink. "I...killed a man."

Trudy Lee paused for a moment. "Just one?"

"See, there you go making fun of me. You don't take me seriously."

Trudy Lee got down on her hands and knees and started wiping up the shake from the floor. "Where's your sense of humor?" Getting no response, she looked up at her and Mona Lee stared her down. "I'm sorry, dear. Go on."

"I was working on this ugly, hot-shot producer."

"Oh my God," Trudy Lee said. But it wasn't her reaction to his being unattractive, it was the uncooked birthday pie, spilled on the floor earlier in the day that had turned to cement that she had forgotten about. She sloshed the vodka smoothie around it, trying to loosen it up. "Housework done properly will kill you."

"Mother, are you listening?"

She stopped scrubbing. "Are you telling me you're a prostitute? 'Cause if you are, I still love you."

"No I am not a prostitute."

She continued to wipe up the mess. "Well, you rub oil on strange men's bodies and get paid for it."

"Shiatsu is done with your clothes on."

"Your clothes?"

Mona Lee shook her head. "Yes, Mother. And the client's."

"That's good to know."

"And no oils are used. But he insisted on being naked, so I threw a sheet over him. He was fat and smelly and I hated every minute of working on him."

Trudy Lee got to her feet and looked down at Mona Lee seriously. "Did he touch you inappropriately?"

"No, and will you let go of the sex stuff?"

Trudy Lee threw the used towels away, grabbed some more and continued cleaning up the floor.

"Mother, it was at the end of the session that I was working on his head. It was the biggest head I've ever seen. It was hard for me to hold it in my hands, never mind lift it. I worked his neck and then was trying to stretch it when it happened."

"What?"

"I dropped it. I dropped his huge, fucking head and I heard something snap, crackle and pop."

Trudy Lee stopped wiping. "Oh dear."

"His eyes opened..."

"Yes?"

"And he said that was the best shiatsu he had ever had, thanked me for the adjustment to his neck and tipped me an extra twenty-five dollars."

Trudy Lee paused and then laughed. "Then what's the problem? You're good at this shatzi stuff." She got up off the floor and continued to wipe down the counters with the paper towels she had been using on the floor.

"It's shiatsu Mother, and I found out the next day that he had died."

Trudy Lee stopped cleaning. "Oh my."

"I got a phone call from the police, 'cause I was in his date book, and they wanted information and all, and I pretended I wasn't me and then threw my clothes into my bag and ran to the airport. It sounds like I may have killed him, doesn't it?"

She started cleaning again. "Sounds like it."

"Mother!"

"I'm sure you'll be cleared of all charges."

"Not if they don't find me."

Trudy Lee stopped wiping. She had to ask the question, but was afraid of the answer. "What do you mean?"

"I'm moving back home."

Trudy Lee spun around and stared at her. "You're what?"

Just then the egg timer went off.

"What's that for?" Mona Lee asked.

"Bert's insulin injection," she said taking off her apron.

"When did he turn diabetic?"

Trudy Lee wiped her brow with her forearm, opened the re-frigerator and took out a vial of insulin. "About a month ago. Come and help me. We'll talk about you moving back home later."

Mona Lee, with the remainder of her shake in hand, followed Trudy Lee down the hallway to Bert's room.

"Mother?"

"Yes?"

"I didn't know that the money I borrowed was for your vaca-tion."

Trudy Lee stopped, turned around and looked at her. There was split second of uncomfortable intimacy. She contemplated touching Mona Lee and then decided against it. "Doesn't matter. Bert would have been too sick to go anyway."

His room was pitch black.

"Bert? Are you awake?" Trudy Lee turned his light on and found him lying on his back. "Time for an injection."

He rolled away from her onto his side.

"Mona Lee, hand me the kit that's over there on the dresser."

She quickly grabbed the black box and handed it to Trudy Lee as though she would catch something from it. "I wish you all had told me had diabetes. I could have worked on his pancreas."

Trudy Lee reached for Bert's arm, but he pulled it away. "You can help his pancreas by giving him his injection."

"I don't know how to do that."

"It doesn't hurt him. Hell, the cancer doesn't even hurt him." She wrestled with him for his hand. "Now Bert, you know I have to test your sugar level. Mona Lee, hold his arm down while I stick his finger into this device."

Mona Lee broke out into a sweat. "I don't feel so good."

"Hell it's just a pin prick." Trudy Lee jabbed Bert's finger into the sugar monitor, which made him jolt. "OK, now in a second it will tell me how much insulin he needs. Hand me a syringe."

Mona Lee's hand shook as she took one out of the kit.

"Dear, if you want to heal people, you're going to have to develop a tougher skin. Speaking of which, pull up your father's shirt."

Mona Lee lifted the pajama top and struggled to get it up over his head.

"No, just expose his stomach."

"Why?"

"That's where you'll inject him."

She put her hand to her mouth. "I'm going to be sick."

"Stop it." Trudy Lee slipped the needle into the vial of insulin, and like a professional, tipped it upside down. She measured out the right amount and then pulled it out. "Hold the needle."

Mona Lee tentatively reached for it as Trudy Lee rubbed an alcohol wipe on his stomach.

"This was so much easier when he had some body fat on his stomach. Damn, look at him. It took cancer to finally give him the washboard stomach I always wanted."

Bert looked up at her.

"Now Mona Lee, pull his skin away and quickly inject the needle."

"But I can't."

"Don't worry, if it goes out through the other side of his skin, we'll just start over."

With that, Mona Lee fainted onto the bed.

"Geez, I have to do everything around here." Trudy Lee stuck the needle into Bert's stomach and he moaned. She injected the insulin, pulled it out, and rubbed the spot with her finger. "There we go Bert. All done." She looked at Mona Lee passed out next to Bert. "Look at this. I've never seen the two of you so close."

Suddenly, Trudy Lee ran out of the room and into the kitchen. She grabbed her camera and rushed back. She positioned Mona Lee's arm so that it was gently touching Bert.

"What a picture." She smiled as the flash went off. She picked up Mona Lee's vodka shake and sipped it as she exited the room, turning out the light.

SEVEN

17,088 HOURS TOO LATE

"Roscoe, you gotta go home." Gus, the bartender at The Neutered Angus, had just given last call.

"One more for the road, Gus?"

"You know your limit. Seven Tom Collinses and that's it my friend. Now, I gotta kick you out. It's closing time."

Roscoe was the only one left in the joint.

"I love you, Gus. Honest I do."

"And I love you too, Roscoe." Gus came around from the back of the bar and helped him off his bar stool. "You gonna make it home OK?"

"Sure. I know the way. Man, you're a good friend, Gus." Roscoe smiled at him as he opened the front door.

"Now, drive safe, you hear?"

"Yea, I hear ya," Roscoe said as he tripped, walking down the front step. "I'll drive safe. But I sure could use one for the road."

Gus closed the door as Roscoe staggered over to his bike. He walked it a few steps and then tried to mount it. His foot slipped off the pedal, he straddled the bar, and fell onto the gravel.

"Ah, fuck! Damn. Shit that hurt!" He picked himself up, mounted the bike again and wobbled off into the darkness.

The Neutered Angus was in Ballardvale, a small village to the east of Ragland. Roscoe focused as hard as he could, and knew that if he just followed the train tracks he'd hit River Road. The last song played on Gus's nostalgic jukebox was *Blues In The Night*, and Roscoe just couldn't seem to get the tune out of his head. He struggled with the lyrics and the notes.

"My mama done told, when I was in knee pants, my mama done told me, son. A woman will get you, and then she'll forget you, to sing the blues in the night."

Suddenly, Roscoe stopped his bike and started crying. "Bunnie! Bunnie Ludlow!"

He made a detour from his route home and pedaled as fast as he could. He rode down Central Street, past South School, past Sid White's Dairy and through the center of Ballardvale. He sailed down the steep slope running alongside the closed sawmill. And at the bottom of the hill, sitting on the banks of the Shawsheen River, he stopped in front of Bunnie Ludlow's house.

She and Roscoe were, secretly high school sweethearts. Secretly, because Trudy Lee had very strong and apparently valid reasons why Roscoe couldn't go near Bunnie. It was always a puzzle to Roscoe why his mother was so set against them sharing the rest of their lives together. The song made him want her more than ever before.

It was after one in the morning and although he was drunk out of his mind, Roscoe had the brains not to ring her doorbell. Instead, he went around to the back of the house she had inherited from her parents, Lorraine and Frank. Sadly, both were killed in a car accident nearly ten years earlier by a drunk driver.

"Bunnie?" he shouted in a whisper. "Bunnie, it's Rosc."

Getting no response, he picked up a stone and threw it up at her bedroom window. It came straight back down and hit him on the head.

"Shit." He then proceeded to climb the trellis that ran up the side of her house. "Bunnie, I'm coming."

He made it up to her open window on the second floor, hung onto the sill and whispered in. "Bunnie, I came back for ya."

She awoke from a deep sleep and wondered if she had dreamt Roscoe's voice. Born in the same year, it was amazing how similar they looked. Both had brown wavy hair, hazel eyes, high cheekbones and strong jaws. In fact, kids in school used to tease them all the time, saying they were long-lost twins.

"Bunnie."

So startled to see him, she did a double take and then tiptoed to the window.

"Roscoe?" she whispered. "Roscoe Martindale, is that you?"

"Yes, Bunnie. I came back."

She looked at her watch. "You're 17,088 hours too late. Are you crazy?"

"Yeah, I'm crazy for you."

Bunnie looked back towards her bed quickly and then grabbed Roscoe's arm. "You ran off with the carnival. I waited two years. You said you would come back for me with at least a million dollars."

Feeling as though he was losing his grip, Roscoe grabbed onto Bunnie's hand. "I almost made the money, but my Pops got sick."

She pulled her hand away from him and he slipped a bit. "I heard. I'm sorry Rosc."

"Damn, I love you so much, Bunnie Ludlow. I want you so bad."

"It's Bunnie Ludlow Bodman, now." She looked back towards her bed again. "You know I married Beufort Bodman."

"Come with me, Bunnie. I know you love me too." He tried to climb in through the window.

Bunnie wrestled with him. "Roscoe, get out. Get out before Beufort kills you. He has a gun and I know he's not afraid to use it." She pushed him back. "Get out now."

"Bun? You awake?" groaned Beufort.

"Yes, Beu. Just closing the window." She kissed Roscoe passionately on the lips. "Roscoe, I'm sorry." She pushed him hard and slammed the window shut, catching one of his fingers.

"Fuck," he whispered, as he fell two stories to the ground. On the way down he tore his shirt on the trellis and landed on a pruned-down rose bush.

A neighbor's dog started barking as Roscoe picked himself up and found his bike. He limped away singing, *"A woman will get you, and then she'll forget you, to sing the blues in the night."*

It was well after two in the morning when Roscoe finally made it back to Terror. He tripped coming up the back stairs to the porch, lost his balance, and broke right through the screen door with his head. Dazed, he staggered through the kitchen door, lost his balance and fell to his knees on the kitchen floor.

With great difficulty he picked himself up and made his way to Bert's room.

"Pop? Pop? Are you in here?"

It took several tries for him to find and turn on the light switch.

"Pop," he shouted stumbling towards him. "Time for a ride."

Roscoe pushed the rocker next to Bert's bed and threw him into it. He dragged the rocker out of the bedroom and banged it into the wall in the hallway.

"Brrrrmmmm! Brrrrmmm! Here we go Pops."

Roscoe zoomed down the hall into the keeping room. Spinning the rocker around, Bert fell out of it and onto the rug.

Roscoe got down on the floor with him. "Pop? You OK, Pop?"

Having heard the commotion, Trudy Lee ran down the back staircase and turned on a light in the keeping room.

"Roscoe? Is that you?"

He struggled to get Bert back into the rocking chair.

"Is your father all right?"

"Where's Lex?" he slurred. "He should be down here with Pop."

"Roscoe, you're drunk." Shaking her head, Trudy Lee went into the kitchen and put the kettle on.

"Ma, he promised he'd cover for me."

"Well, if you hadn't run out like that, you'd know that he got the worst migraine of his life."

Slivered memories of the birthday dinner came back to him. "I'm not surprised."

"Roscoe, we all thought he was having a stroke." She came back into the keeping room and looked at him more closely. "Your shirt's torn. And your eye! What's happened to you? Were you in a fight?"

"Noooo. Ssssshhhh! Mother I want you to sit here." He pushed her onto the loveseat.

"Roscoe."

"Mommy, I love you so much. I do." He swung his head around and looked at Bert. "And Daddy, I love you too."

Bert just stared at him as Trudy Lee started to get up out of the loveseat. "We love you too, dear."

He pushed her back rather violently. "No, stay! Sit, Mother! Stay! God, I miss Bob."

Frightened, Trudy Lee sat on the loveseat as Roscoe stumbled into the kitchen. "Roscoe, what are you doing?"

He took the liquor bottles from the cabinet beneath the bread-box. He gathered them up in his arms and walked back to Trudy Lee and Bert.

"I know you didn't know I knew where they were. But wasn't I good? I didn't drink from them at all."

They just watched him in disbelief as he lined the bottles up in a semi-circle in front of them and then sat down on the floor.

"Mommy? Daddy? I want to share with you what I've shared with all of Alaska. What'll you have?" He gestured to the bottles of liquor. "I can make 'em all. It's on the house."

"Please Roscoe," begged Trudy Lee. "I'm sure you were a wonderful bartender."

"The best!"

"Yes, darling but…"

"I was, Mommy. I was the best." He climbed up onto the love-seat with her. "And you're the best, mommy." He made little kissing sounds. "The best mommy in the world." He kissed her neck.

"And you're the best son."

"Better than Lex?" He tried to kiss her romantically on the lips, but Trudy Lee pushed him away. Bert stared at them as the teakettle began to whistle.

"Please! Stop! Roscoe! Stop it!"

Hearing the kettle and her screams, Lex ran down the back stairs and over to Trudy Lee and Roscoe.

"Help! Lex, get your brother off me!"

Lex peeled Roscoe away from Trudy Lee. "Come on, Rosc. Calm down."

Roscoe looked at all of them, stumbled towards the stairs, and then sat down on the bottom step.

"What happened to you, Roscoe?" Lex then ran into the kitchen and turned off the whistling teakettle.

Trudy Lee pulled herself together and dragged the rocker and Bert down the hall to the bathroom, as Lex went back to Roscoe.

"Hey, big brother. Happy Birthday. I love you, Lex. I really do."

Lex grabbed him under his arms. "I love you too, Roscoe. Now let's get you to bed."

"But I don't like the Midge. Is that OK? Am I a despic…am I a dispic…am I an awful person?"

"No Rosc. You're not awful."

He violently pushed Lex away. "I can make it on my own. Let me climb the stairs on my own. I can do it. I know I can."

Roscoe got down on all fours, and, even stinking drunk, he knew to skip over the fourth step. Lex watched him as he made the slow climb to the top and then disappeared.

"He wants his beer and cigarettes," Trudy Lee she said as she dried her hands on a towel.

Lex went into the kitchen and got the beer out of the fridge, while Trudy Lee pulled cigarettes out of the kitchen drawer.

"Tea?" Lex asked.

"Please dear," she whispered as she headed back to the bathroom.

Lex dropped tea bags into the two mugs and poured the water. He then went into the keeping room, picked up the liquor bottles, and took them back into the kitchen.

Exhausted, Trudy Lee came out of the bathroom. "Let's sit in the salon."

Lex carried the tea as he followed her down to the front room. With a few embers still burning in the fireplace, Trudy Lee threw a log on, stoked the fire, and then joined him on the divan.

"Lex? I don't know. Between Roscoe and Mona Lee, I just don't know what I did wrong."

"What about Junior?"

"Gee, thanks."

He took a sip of his tea. "What is his problem?"

"He's married to it. Heaven knows why he would pick such a domineering wife."

Lex suppressed a smile, knowing exactly why he had chosen Clairese. "He doesn't speak anymore."

"Like father, like son."

They both sipped and watched the fire for a few moments. "So Roscoe's drinking again?"

"That boy needs to learn how to blow off steam in a healthy way."

Not sure if he really wanted to know the answer, Lex had to ask. "What was he doing to you?"

"He...um...your brother was trying to...kiss me." They looked at each other very seriously and then started to laugh. "He wanted to play bartender for your father and me."

They laughed harder, and then Trudy Lee started to cry.

Lex let her have a moment and gazed at the fire. "I'm sorry, Mother."

She brushed away tears. "Oh, sometimes I wish I was never born."

"But then I wouldn't be here. And aren't you the one who always said you mustn't wish your life away?"

She shook her head. "Your life, Lex, not mine."

"When this is all over, you need to find yourself a hunky young man with lots of money."

She smiled devilishly. "How about a sexy young woman with lots of money? I'm tired of men."

"Mother!"

They laughed and sipped their tea as the fire crackled.

"I feel so bad," Lex said frowning.

Trudy Lee felt his forehead. "Your migraine?"

"No, that's easing up. It's my birthday wish. I wished..."

She put her fingertips to his lips. "Oh, you mustn't tell or it won't come true."

Lex held her hand and looked at her. "Good. I wished that Daddy would die before I had to watch him tonight."

She was quiet for a bit. "I understand, Lex. I've wished the same."

"It just frightens me so. Seeing him suffer and waste away like this. It seems like such a horrible way to end a life."

"It is. And it just reminds me of how scared I am of dying, being excommunicated and all."

Lex wasn't sure if he had heard her correctly. "When did that happen?"

She responded quite nonchalantly. "When I got divorced and then remarried."

She sipped her tea as he stared at her. "Excuse me?"

"The Catholic Church doesn't recognize divorce, but the big sin is remarrying."

"I'm aware of their very Christian ideals but wait a minute.

Who were you married to?"

She nervously played with the belt to her bathrobe. "I must have told you."

"Mother, I think I'd remember."

"He was the most gorgeous man in the world. I named you after him."

Lex choked on his tea.

"Well, kind of. His name was Aleksander. And he's your sister's father."

Lex nearly fell off the divan. "I beg your pardon?"

"I was pregnant when we divorced. I married your father four weeks later."

Lex turned to face her. "Mother, you're joking?"

She shook her head.

"But does Daddy know?"

"He must. Your sister's growth wasn't stunted by hormone shots. Her real father was a shrimp. A gorgeous, Cuban shrimp."

Lex looked back at the fire with disbelief. "You aren't going to say anything now, are you?"

She touched his arm. "I was thinking that if I told your sister the truth, maybe it would make us closer."

Lex honestly had no idea if she was telling the truth or not. But what was predictable was that when her integrity was questioned, she was more than likely to retaliate with exaggerated lies. So whether it was true or not, it was imperative that Mona Lee not find out if Trudy Lee sincerely wanted to be closer to her daughter.

He gave her a sarcastic look. "Trust me Mother, do not tell her. It would not bring the two of you closer."

"No?"

"I can't believe you were married before."

"Oh, get over it. I did."

They paused as a log slipped off the grate. Lex got up and wedged it back up with the poker. "Mother, does Daddy love me?"

"Of course he does. Why would you ask such a question?"

He came back to Trudy Lee and sat at her feet. "Because he's never said it to me."

Trudy Lee laughed hard. "Join the club. He's never said it to me, either."

He looked up at her seriously. "Do you know that I have never seen you and Daddy kiss or hold hands? Ever."

"That's because we never did. The poor guy was so frightened of intimacy. It's a wonder we had you two boys."

"Mother, that's three boys," Lex laughed. "You had three boys."

"Three," she said, quickly covering herself. "Of course."

"How did you and Daddy meet?"

"You must know."

"Honestly, you never told me."

"1949. A dance at town hall. American Tobacco Company sponsored the socials, hoping to get in good with the citizens of Ragland. I'll never forget. Your father was the only one there reading a book."

"I can believe that."

"Oh, but he was so handsome. Looked just like Clark Gable."

"Really?"

"No. Daddy looked better," Trudy Lee smiled. "And I walked myself right over to him and asked if we could have a dance. I think he trembled the whole time."

Lex smiled. "Do you love him?"

"In a safe kind of way. Bert offered me security, but Aleksander offered me passion."

"So why did you divorce him?"

"I wasn't in love with Aleksander."

"Then why did you get married?"

Her brow furrowed. "To get away from Grandma Battles."

"Mother, why would you ever want to do that?" Lex asked incredulously.

"Oh darling," Trudy Lee sighed as she ran her fingers through his hair. "My mother's remarks are a barrel of laughs now, but did you ever stop to imagine what it would be like to have her as a mother?"

Lex pondered that one. "I can't say that I have."

"First of all, she resented the fact that I showed up so soon after her marrying Grandpa Battles. Once she became pregnant, she had to stay at home while Papa toured with the soccer team. Trust me, she wasn't a happy camper."

"But she sure has a great sense of humor."

"Yeah, at my expense. And things only got worse as I became a teenager."

* * * *

In June of 1944, Trudy Lee Battles was eighteen-years-old and America was in the middle of World War II. Papa Battles, having served in World War I, was exempt from doing duty. And as was usually the case, the economy was doing well during wartime. Just about everyone in the States could get a job.

Papa Battles had long since retired from playing soccer, and although he and Anastasia both were working in factories, making metal parts for fighter planes, they just never seemed to have enough money.

Trudy Lee grew up in a shotgun house that sat on a very small parcel of land on top of Blue Hill, situated in the northeast corner of Ragland. It was called a shotgun house because, if you opened the front door and shot a gun straight into the house, the bullet would exit out the back door without hitting anything.

The house was built in 1906 and was one room wide and four deep. All of the rooms were off the central hallway. The living room was in the front. Anastasia and Papa Battles' bedroom was next, followed by Trudy Lee's, and, as was typical, the kitchen was in the back.

One drawback with this type of home was that there was virtually no privacy at all. Of course, Papa Battles would close Trudy Lee's door before he and Anastasia made love, and both parents convinced each other of their daughter's always sleeping like a rock. However, the truth was that, more times than not, she could hear every peep, sigh and moan that came from her parents' bedroom.

Many times as a child, late at night, Trudy Lee would creep onto the quaint little porch outside the front door to escape their ecstasy. Sitting in the rocking chair, counting as many shooting stars as she could, she'd make wish after wish, hoping that someday soon she'd find the man of her dreams too.

The outside of the house was painted a forest green. And speaking of green, that's exactly the type of thumb Papa Battles had. He did remarkable work with the shrubbery and flowerbeds around the property. He even planted a vegetable garden out back each year, which, during the summer months, produced zucchini, sweet corn, tomatoes, string beans, three types of lettuce, and Trudy Lee's favorite, watermelon.

And although it certainly was not considered the slums, the house was definitely situated on the wrong side of the tracks. Anastasia did everything in her power to make what she called The Bungalow as charming and inviting as she could. Each of the rooms was painted a cheery color. She found attractive, second-hand furniture, and even some nice antiques at local thrift stores. And having learned how to sew at an early age, she made beautiful curtains for all the windows.

To her daughter's dismay, all of her clothes had to be handmade too.

"Honestly, Trudy Lee, one would think you were born with a silver spoon in your mouth," exclaimed Anastasia as she pinned the side seam of her thick wool skirt. Trudy Lee, without letting her friends know, had found the used suit at the Salvation Army.

"Dorothy Sundry and Eleanor Bates wouldn't be caught dead

in homemade clothes," sulked Trudy Lee. "They're classy. They bought their tailored suits from the Sears and Roebuck mail catalogue."

"Yeah, real classy," mumbled Anastasia. "Why in God's name do you insist on wearing a wool suit in June? You'll die of heat stroke."

"Because that's what Betty wears."

"Betty who? Boop?"

"Very funny, Mother. Betty Bacall."

"You mean Lauren?"

"Yes. But I read in Movie Star Magazine that her real name is Betty. That's what her friends and family call her."

Anastasia spun Trudy Lee around. "Oh, so now we're on a first name basis with movie stars?"

"And she wears a tailored suit in *To Have And Have Not* with Bogie and she's absolutely stunning."

Before focusing on Marilyn Monroe, Trudy Lee was obsessed with Lauren Bacall.

"Well, Trudy Lee Battles, at a dance in Ragland, North Carolina, on a sweltering night in June wearing a heavy wool suit, you're going to look more sweaty than stunning."

"Dorothy and Eleanor wouldn't be caught dead going to a dance at the November Club."

Exasperated, Anastasia looked up at her daughter. "Now what's wrong with the November Club?"

"Old fogies show up there, Mother," Trudy Lee exclaimed as she shifted weight from one foot to the other, while standing on an orange crate.

"Stop your fidgeting or I'll poke you with a pin, young lady. Those spoiled girls don't know what living on a budget means."

"Of course not. They all have money to burn, Mother."

"Nonsense. No one has that much money," remarked Anastasia, annoyed and wanting to change the subject. "And if you hadn't gained so much weight, you could have fit into one of my dresses."

Anastasia didn't need to poke Trudy Lee with a pin, she was doing just fine with her words. And the truth is, Trudy Lee was never overweight. She just had a very mature, hourglass figure, one that she blossomed into at the early age of thirteen. What Anastasia Battles could never acknowledge was that she was actually envious of Trudy Lee's looks.

"And I wouldn't be surprised if these girls were imaginary friends," Anastasia continued.

Trudy Lee looked down at her, shocked. "Mother, why would you say that?"

"Because you've never invited them over."

"Well, of course not. I don't want them to see how we live."

"That's it!" Anastasia shouted slamming her sewing box shut. "I'm through!"

"But my seam isn't stitched and my skirt isn't hemmed."

"If you are that ashamed of the way we live, then do your own damn sewing, Trudy Lee Battles!" And with that, Anastasia stormed out of the living room, down the hallway, through the kitchen and out the back door.

"Mother!" Trudy Lee hollered, as she made her way to the back of the house.

Anastasia sat herself down on the swing beneath the old oak tree, with her back to the house. Trudy Lee was tempted to apologize to her, but on second thought decided to go back inside and finish getting ready.

Maybe if their house had been bigger, or maybe if Papa Battles didn't have to work double shifts to make enough money to survive, and was home more often, or maybe if Anastasia could have had more children, maybe, just maybe, mother and daughter wouldn't have been at each other's throats constantly.

But just having graduated from high school, and aching to spread her wings and fly out into the world, Trudy Lee was desperate to start her own life. And Anastasia was more than eager to push her voluptuous chick out of the nest.

Looking at her watch, Anastasia came back into the house and threw on a simple yet elegant dress that, of course, she had made for herself.

Meanwhile, Trudy Lee struggled with the sewing. She haphazardly stitched together the side seam and simply taped the hem of her skirt an inch and a half higher than Anastasia would have allowed. And with silk stockings nowhere to be found, she hastily slopped on Max Factor's pancake make-up onto her legs. She removed the curlers from her head and combed out her shoulder-length chestnut brown hair. She then slipped into her much-too-high, second-hand leather pumps, coated her lips with another layer of Revlon's brilliant red Fire and Ice lipstick that matched her fingernail polish, and mother and daughter headed out the door.

"You forgot your blouse," screamed Anastasia as she looked at Trudy Lee.

"Mother, she doesn't wear one."

"She?"

"Betty," exclaimed Trudy Lee. "She always wears her suit jackets without a blouse."

Any other time Anastasia would have had made Trudy Lee change and scrape the make-up off her face, but they were late for the dance. And come hell or high water, Anastasia Battles was determined to find her daughter a man that night.

Papa Battles had their only car with him at the night shift, so they had to make the two-and-a-half mile trip in ninety-six degree, with full humidity, weather, on foot.

"Stop walking like a truck driver, Trudy Lee," snapped Anastasia as she looked at her watch. "We're late as it is."

"Mother, it's these shoes. We're going too fast."

"Just bend your knees a little."

Trudy Lee bent her knees, which forced her butt out and her upper body to lean forward. Anastasia let her daughter walk ahead of her a bit and then she just couldn't help but break down laughing.

"What?" asked Trudy Lee spinning around, just knowing she was going to make fun of her. "What? What's wrong with me?"

Anastasia couldn't tell her what she was really thinking.

"Oh dear, there's nothing wrong with you. I was just remembering something amusing I heard on the radio earlier today. Truly, you look…fine."

Trudy Lee eyed her suspiciously and then continued to walk on with bent knees. Strutting down the road like Groucho Marx in drag, Anastasia doubled over in silent laughter, as they made their way to the November Club.

By the time Anastasia and Trudy Lee reached their destination they were no longer perspiring. Both were drenched in sweat. Granted, most of the walk was down hill, but the last turn they had to make to get to the Club was a left onto Black Crow Road, which felt to them, on this extremely moist day, as though it were straight up.

Out of breath, Anastasia checked Trudy Lee before heading into the dance.

"Mother, it sounds like a big band," Trudy Lee squealed, all out of breath as she pushed back a dark brown curl dangling over her forehead. "Do you think they really have a big band in there?"

"Sounds like it," Anastasia mumbled trying to curb her own enthusiasm. "Turn around, dear. Hmmm."

"What? What? What does hmmmm, mean, Mother?"

"Nothing. You look fine." But in truth, Anastasia thought her daughter looked absolutely stunning. And with that, Anastasia marched her way up to the front door of the social club with her daughter trailing behind her.

Trudy Lee was right; the November Club was usually full of old fogies, and Anastasia knew it. But in her mind she thought that an old fogy was much more likely to have a steady job and an interest in marrying than a young stud.

The stark room was crowded with women of all ages, shapes and sizes. And peppered here and there were a few older men and some younger ones, who, in the eyes of the United States Armed Services, were defective.

In the midst of a sloppy rendition of *Chattanooga Choo Choo*, Anastasia disappeared into the sea of high-decibel-chirping women, leaving Trudy Lee to fend for herself. So naturally, she ran to the food table. And while inhaling an assortment of cheese cubes, and fanning her sweltering body, Trudy Lee Battles met Aleksander Cortez Martinez, aka Leks.

"Hell-lo," he said in a very thick Cuban accent.

Trudy Lee turned around and saw no one. Thinking it was an echo of music bouncing around in the cavernous hall, she focused back on the food table.

Leks took another stab at making a connection as Trudy Lee stabbed a stuffed olive with a toothpick.

"Would the pretty lady like to dance?"

Trudy Lee looked back in the direction from which his voice had come. She glanced straight out, to the left and then to the right.

"Please?" he asked in the most scrumptious accent.

Trudy Lee finally looked down. Standing beneath her was a very short, but beautiful Latin hunk. Her jaw dropped and her olive promptly fell out of her mouth and hit him on the forehead.

"Ah geez," she cried, wiping his forehead with her hand. "I'm sorry."

"It's perfectly all right. Would you like to dance with me?" He was twenty-five, and had the most luscious wavy black hair, full red lips, cleft chin and deep-sea-green eyes.

Thrown but delighted, Trudy Lee answered, "Yes."

The music suddenly changed as Aleksander guided her to the middle of the dance floor. The band picked up with, appropriately enough, *Begin The Beguine*.

Although Trudy Lee had never had formal dance lessons, she

was a natural. And any free moment they found, Dorothy Sundry would have Eleanor Bates and Trudy Lee over to her house, and they'd practice dancing to records. The problem was, Trudy Lee being the biggest of the three, she was always delegated to dancing the male part. The lead.

At first it was hard for Aleksander and Trudy Lee to find their rhythm, but once she relaxed and let him take charge, the dance floor seemed to open up, and everyone watched from the sides. They were quite the pair. A gorgeous Trudy Lee towering over Aleksander, who was reeking of sex appeal.

Midway through the tropical song, Anastasia wrestled her way to the front lines to witness what everyone was gawking at, and was astonished to see her daughter dancing with the charming Cuban cutie.

Struck with conflicting emotions, Anastasia strode out onto the dance floor and promptly cut in.

"May the mother have a dance?"

Anastasia literally pushed Trudy Lee out of Aleksander's arms and started gliding along the dance floor with him. She never could resist a strong flirt. And while they were dancing, Anastasia cemented some sort of agreement with Aleksander Cortez Martinez and strongly encouraged him to court her daughter.

Humiliated that her mother had taken over, Trudy Lee mustered her strength and marched back up to them. She made two attempts at butting in, and then she saw it. And it was the first time she had seen it all night. With a Cheshire cat grin on her face, Trudy Lee poked at her mother's back.

"Mother?" she interrupted.

Anastasia ignored her.

"Mother!" she shouted.

"Yes, Trudy Lee, what is it?" asked Anastasia waving at her as though she were an annoying mosquito.

"Mother, I was dancing with him and…"

"And what?"

"And your dress is inside out," Trudy Lee laughed.

Anastasia stopped dancing immediately and looked at what she was wearing. And as she brought attention to it, everyone else in the dance hall noticed, too. In her horror, she spun around in circles looking at all the exposed seams. What Anastasia hadn't realized, in her haste to get ready, was that she had slipped her dress on inside out. The frayed edges suddenly made the classic black cocktail dress look like a feedbag.

Mortified, she dashed out of the November Club and ran all the way home. Meanwhile, Trudy Lee continued dancing with Aleksander Cortez Martinez. But somewhere between *You Go To My Head* and *Just In Time*, she started having her own problems with her suit. First the tape on the hem became unstuck. Then as Aleksander twirled Trudy Lee, the side seam came undone and created a sexy slit all the way up to her hip. And due to all of her perspiring, the pancake make-up on her legs started to run, streaking them orange and white.

But she was having the time of her life with a sexy foreigner, so she couldn't have cared less what anyone else thought as she left the dance club that fateful June night, and slipped into Aleksander's sleek new 1944 Oldsmobile. Trudy Lee Battles and Aleksander Cortez Martinez were promptly married two weeks later.

* * * *

"My very own Ricky Ricardo, Lex."

There was a moment of silence. It was so clear to him that Trudy Lee was a carbon copy of Anastasia. And Mona Lee was the copy of her. The frightening realization was that as each generation progressed, the copies became more dysfunctional, like a photograph that has been reproduced too many times.

"Amazing, Mother. What did Aleksander do for a living?"

"Export/import something from Cuba. I'm sure whatever it was, it was illegal. Anyway, Aleksander was my chance to get away from my mother. And Bert was my chance to get away from Aleksander."

"Why did you divorce Aleksander?"

"We went on a romantic honeymoon to Niagara Falls...."

"So Marilyn."

"Thank you very much. But unlike Ricky Ricardo, Aleksander didn't play the drums. He played me. To the hilt. And started beating up on me."

"Hitting you? My God! But you stayed married to him for...?"

"Five years, Lex."

"Why, Mother, why?"

"It's hard to explain, dear," she said as she thought back. "Aleksander was very powerful, almost hypnotic. And more often than not, he talked me into believing that I deserved to be hit."

He touched her hand. "I'm so sorry."

"It was only in hindsight that I realized he married me to become a United States citizen. One good thing that came out of meeting him was that he persuaded me to go blonde." Trudy Lee primped her hair. "But why he hated me so much I'll never know. Maybe it was because I was a foot taller than he was."

Lex laughed. "Was he an alcoholic?"

"No. I couldn't even blame it on that. I just think he was one of those masochists."

"You mean a misogynist?"

"No. I mean a woman hater."

Lex smiled and thought of Mattie Lee.

"He broke my arm in three places the night I left him."

"Mother, I had no idea!" Lex said horrified.

"I've had trouble typing ever since. Ruined my secretarial career."

He sat next to her, looking at her face. "You were so beautiful, you should have been an actress."

"I did have the lead in my high school play. But you are the actor in the family."

"Was. And I don't miss it one bit."

She nudged him. "I play your commercials all the time for all my friends."

"Mother, it was just one commercial. And you've got to stop exaggerating my accomplishments. Are you telling people my book is reaching the bestseller list? I told you the publisher canned the project. It's off until my agent finds another house."

"I know. I know. It's just that I want to see you succeed so bad."

"But by exaggerating what I have done, you make me feel like I'm not doing well enough."

"Oh, I'm so sorry Lex. I'd never mean to do that."

Suddenly, a spark popped and the log rolled over in the fireplace. It had just dawned on Lex that this was the first time in hours that he hadn't thought about his own life-threatening situation. There was a pause and Lex looked as though he were about to cry.

"Lex honey, I said I was sorry."

"It's not that." He sensed this was the moment to tell Trudy Lee. He just didn't know how to bring it up. "I was just thinking of my life and my friends. Most of them are either dead or dying."

Trudy Lee ran her fingers through his hair again and he smiled.

"Mother, sometimes I imagine myself, after I'm dead, sitting at a little table in a charming café, up on a cloud, sipping a smart cocktail. And an angel is sitting there next to me and asks, 'So, how did you like it?' And I ask, 'Like what?' And the angel says, 'Life.' And I pause to think and the only response I have is, 'The food was good.'"

Trudy Lee laughed.

"I mean I've met some nice people and been to some beautiful places, but if I had the chance to do it all over again, I wouldn't. It's too painful."

"Oh Lex, darling. You mustn't worry yourself with such

thoughts. You're going to be around for a long, long time and be rich and famous, and all the pain will go away."

"Mother, there's something I've been wanting to talk to you about."

Just then, Bert flushed the toilet.

"Hold that thought, dear. Nature's calling."

Frustrated, Lex got up and followed Trudy Lee back to the bathroom. He watched his mother and father from the doorway.

"OK, Bert. Are you all done with your business?" He nodded and reached out for her arm. "Let's get you back into bed. Here, Lex, you'd better lift him."

Lex went into the bathroom as Trudy Lee headed to the kitchen. Having never really touched his father before, there was the slightest hesitation before he put his arms around him. Shocked at how light he was, Lex chose to carry him to the maid's room, as opposed to sliding him in the rocker.

Lex gently placed Bert back into bed, brought the covers up and tucked him in. He was just about to leave, but then stopped and looked at his father. Bert stared back at him. No words spoken, Lex felt his father say thank you. Lex's eyes began to mist and he quickly turned out the light and left the room.

He paused a moment, before joining Trudy Lee, to wipe away the tears.

"Lex, I don't know what I'd ever do without you. You're the only one I can really talk to. Dear, what was it you wanted to tell me?"

He paused, looked at her and gave her a loving embrace.

"Just how much I love you."

Arm-in-arm, they walked up the stairs together, stepping over the fourth step.

EIGHT

THE CHILD OF SATAN

His headache still lingering and unable to sleep, Lex tossed and turned on the too-soft twin mattress in the upstairs back bedroom. Roscoe, with whom he was sharing the room, had passed out on his bed fully-clothed and was snoring loudly. Lex looked at his watch, which read 3:37 AM. He got out of bed and decided to get dressed.

He put on his black turtleneck and pants, but hesitated to wear his Prada shoes. Lex looked over at Roscoe's feet. Gingerly, he pulled off his work boots and slipped into them. Their being a size too big, he laced up the tops to keep them from falling off.

Lex tiptoed down the hallway. He looked into Grandma Battles' room where she appeared to be fast asleep. Across the hall he could hear Mona Lee talking gibberish in her sleep. He thought she blurted out something like, "Not guilty!" as he closed her door. In the front bedroom, Trudy Lee was in a deep sleep, wearing her pink sleeping mask and earplugs.

Lex descended the back staircase to the kitchen. He quietly walked down to Bert's room and listened at the door. He could hear his labored breathing.

He then went to the front salon and checked to see that the embers were out in the fireplace. Knowing all was safe and sound in Terror, he went to the front door, lifted the handle up with all his strength and then squeaked the door opened. He almost closed it, leaving a crack open. He ran across the veranda, flew down the front steps and out across the front lawn.

Assuming all would be asleep, Lex was very excited to see that a light was still on in the Lovejoy house next door. With almost a full moon above, Lex could easily see his way over and was eager to do a little peeping.

He climbed over the stone wall that separated their properties and stealthily made his way to the front of the Lovejoy's house. Much larger than Terror, their red brick house was built at the turn of the century. Sadly, the Lovejoys had bought the house as a foreclosure, and having no money to speak of had let this Victorian beauty fall into decay.

Lex was making his way across the front of their property when he tripped over a piece of old slate that was buckling up along the walkway. He fell to his left knee tearing a hole in his pants.

"Shit," he whispered.

He waited a moment to see if anyone had heard him, and then he crept to the window where the light was on. Someone was alone in the front room. Lex strained his eyes to make out who it was.

Wearing a bra and panties, black stockings and a garter belt, the blonde long-haired person was dancing. He knew it had to be Betsy, even though she looked a bit hefty. Mildly disgusted, Lex was just about to leave when the woman turned around.

Lex's jaw dropped. It was Delbert in drag.

"Oh my God," screamed Lex. "You fucking moron."

Delbert stopped dancing and looked towards the window. Half laughing, half panicking, Lex crouched down beneath the sill as it started to rain again.

Delbert opened the window and looked out as Lex held his breath. He closed it and turned out the light in the front room. Lex stood up when all of a sudden he heard the front door open.

"Hello," shouted Delbert. "Amory?"

Amory? Who's that?

"Somebody out there?"

Lex froze until Delbert closed the door. Relieved, he decided to make his way back home.

"Yes," Lex whispered. "I got you, you fucking moron. Damn, if only I had had mother's camera."

Suddenly, a Rottweiler came charging from the back of the house towards Lex.

"Holy shit," he cried. As fast as he could, Lex ran to the stone wall. He stepped up onto it, but caught his right foot between two stones. He yanked, and Roscoe's boot fell off as he tumbled over to the other side. Lex reached for it, but the dog snatched it up in his mouth.

Lex ran up his driveway with the dog nipping at his heels. Thinking fast, he made a sharp right and, quicker than a cat, he climbed up the rickety two-by-fours to his old tree house. Or what was left of it, which were just a few planks of wood perilously dangling across two limbs.

The Rottweiler ran to the base of the tree. Frustrated and angry, he barked at Lex while trying to shinny up after him.

A light came back on in the Lovejoy house as Lex trembled on the platform, clinging to the tree.

"Amory?" Delbert called out from the front door. "Amory, get in here!"

"What kind of stupid name is that for a dog?" whispered Lex.

Amory growled at him.

"Sorry. Nice dog. Nice Amory."

"Amory!" shouted Delbert once more, but the dog wouldn't budge. He closed the door and turned out the light.

Lex spent the rest of the night up in the tree house, in the rain.

*　*　*　*

A little after seven in the morning, frozen to the bone and soaking wet, Lex crept up to Terror's front door, minus Roscoe's work boot. Amory had finally gone home to have breakfast, with the shoe. Someone in the course of the night had closed the front door. Fearing he would draw attention to himself by trying to open it, he ran around to the back of the house.

Just as he was about to squeak open the screen door, Lex heard a bloodcurdling scream come from the Slaves' Quarters.

"Aaaaaahhhhhhh!"

He registered it as Clairese's annoying pitch and then ran into Terror.

Lex checked the kitchen, dining room and front salon to see whether or not anyone was downstairs. With the coast clear, he tiptoed up the front double staircase, but sneezed as he reached the top landing. He paused to see if anyone had heard him.

Trudy Lee was humming in her bedroom as he passed quietly by. Mona Lee's door was closed, as was Grandma Battles'. Roscoe was still passed out on his bed as Lex looked into the bedroom. He grabbed some fresh clothes from his bag and ran into the bathroom.

He stripped down and let the hot water from the shower cleanse him, not only of the dirt, but also of the sheer stupidity of the night before.

Clairese let out another hair-raising scream. "Aaaaaahhhhhhh! Mattie Lee Martindale? Get yourself into this kitchen right now!"

Mattie Lee was sitting in their upstairs bathroom, cradling her stomach. Like Lex, she hadn't slept a wink all night. Fearing her mother more than God, she didn't know how to tell her parents that she was pregnant.

"They're going to kill me," she whispered to herself. "And if I confess that the father is a Lovejoy, I'm certain they'll reciprocate me and kill me again."

Junior, with vacuum in hand, came running to see what was wrong with Clairese. "What's all the…"

"It's awful," she screamed cutting him off. "It's pure sin."

Hearing that, Mattie Lee wondered how her mother could have found out. She thought about running away, but didn't know where to go. With only $35.18 to her name, Mattie Lee knew it wouldn't take her far. She slowly opened the bathroom door and ran to her bedroom.

"What is the matter Clairese?" Junior asked.

She handed him a booklet.

"Read this. Read what is in Mattie Lee's Bible class workbook."

Junior grabbed it. "Well I'm assuming they are the teachings of…"

"Satan!" screamed Clairese. "We have spawned the child of Satan is all I can say. Read! Read her lessons on page 27. Look how she has answered the questions."

Junior turned to page 27. "Chapter 14. The Book of Matthew, questions over verses 13-21. Question 1: How many did Jesus feed?"

Junior looked at Clairese.

"Go on. Go on and read her answer."

"Answer: Jesus fed…40,000,000." Junior frowned. "Is that wrong?"

"Go on!"

"Question 2: What did He use to feed them? Answer: Meatloaf." Junior instantly bit his lip, suppressing a laugh.

Clairese was about to burst a blood vessel. "Read the next one!"

"Question 3: How much was left over?" Junior made all sorts of odd faces trying not to smile. "Answer: All of it."

Junior knew very well that Mattie Lee was referring to Clairese's meatloaf, which the two of them secretly referred to as her "brickloaf."

"And the best one yet," yelled Clairese.

"Question 4: What does this teach you about His power? Answer: He was a terrible cook?" Starting to snicker, Junior covered himself and turned it into hysterical coughing.

"Mattie Lee Martindale! Get your good for nothing, you're going to wish you were never born, I'm going to give you something to really cry about, sorry little...behind down here, right now," hollered her mother.

Junior tried to leave but Clairese grabbed his arm. "Continue," she ordered.

"There's more?"

"You better believe it!"

"Questions over verses 22-33. Question 1. Why were the disciples afraid when they saw Jesus? Answer: Cause he wore stripes with plaids."

"Blasphemy," she yelled.

"Ah, come on Clairese. She's just..."

"Read on!"

"Question 2. What did Peter want to do?" Junior looked up at the ceiling, afraid of the answer. He took a deep breath and continued. "Peter wanted to...fly off to never never land." Junior put his forearm up to his mouth to hide his smile. "Question 3. What happened when Peter took his eyes off Christ? Answer: Christ dated Wendy."

"Whose child wrote this?" asked Clairese. "This isn't ours. Someone must have switched babies at birth. She can't be of our creation."

"Question 4. How will we be saved like Peter? Answer: By clapping our hands."

"The fifth one?"

"Question 5. What did they say when Christ got into the boat? Answer: Sit down, sit down, sit down, sit down, sit down you're rockin' the boat."

"And the piece de resistance...read the last one!"

"The last question of the lesson: Please name the Holy Trinity.

Answer: The Father, the Son and the Holy…"

"No don't say it!" Clairese screamed dropping her head into her hands.

"Oh my," Junior squealed as he turned away laughing.

"Mattie Lee, get down stairs, now," ordered Clairese.

Mattie Lee opened her bedroom door and slowly worked her way down the stairs. Tears had stained what Clairese called her cleaning sweat suit. The one that matched the ones both of her parents were wearing.

Having reached the bottom step, and seeing how angry her mother was, Mattie Lee tried to make a dash to the door. Clairese charged after her, allowing Junior to fall apart in hysterics.

"What in God's name were you thinking?" she asked grabbing her shoulders.

Assuming her anger was over her pregnancy, Mattie Lee responded, "It all happened so fast."

"I'm taking you down to Father Ken and he is going to rid you of this evil, evil…thing…inside of you."

"Father Ken?" she asked confused and frightened.

"Yes," screamed Clairese. "I was wrong. Trudy Lee isn't the one who should be exorcised. It's you."

"Me, Mother?"

"He'll exorcise you of the devil that is lodged deep within your existence!"

"Daddy?" Mattie Lee cried.

He managed to put on a serious face. "Mattie Lee. You did sin."

"But…but…it's not all my fault," she confessed.

"So there's an accomplice here?" asked Clairese.

"See Clairese," Junior said, "Mattie Lee didn't do it on her own."

"Of course not, Daddy. Lowell Lovejoy had the…"

"So he's one?" Clairese hollered cutting her off.

"Yes. Well…we…did it…together in the chicken coop."

"I'm burning it down this afternoon. As soon as Father Ken cleanses your body and soul. Is that understood?"

"How will he do it, Mother," she cried.

"I haven't the foggiest idea. But I'm sure the process will be long and painful."

Mattie Lee cried harder as she held her stomach.

Clairese continued. "While I call to make the appointment, the two of you…back to cleaning!"

Junior plugged the cord into the kitchen outlet and started vacuuming. Mattie Lee, crying her eyes out, picked up a dust rag.

Across the way in Terror, Anastasia, wearing a bright green pantsuit, opened her bedroom window and stuck her hand out.

"Damn, it always rains when I come to this dreary place."

She closed the window and made her way over to a chair next to the bed. She slipped on her galoshes, stood up and put on her raincoat and hat. She grabbed her handbag and walked out of her bedroom.

Anastasia scurried along the upstairs hall, bounced down the staircase to the kitchen, hopped over the fourth step and then grabbed a kitchen chair. She dragged it over to the back porch door and plopped herself down. She sat there patiently for at least fifteen minutes before Lex came down into the kitchen with a bottle of pills.

Not noticing his grandmother, he went over to the sink and poured himself a glass of water. He opened the bottle and took out one pill. He grabbed a tablespoon, placed the pill in it, and with the flat end of another spoon, he crushed the tablet into a powder. He then sprinkled a little sugar on it and very carefully dripped a few drops of water over the powder. With the tip of the spoon he stirred the mixture, took a deep breath and slid it into his mouth. He took a quick gulp of water and swallowed it down.

"Yuck."

"Good morning Lex," Anastasia said still sitting by the door.

Lex spun around, knocking the bottle of pills over. One

dropped to the kitchen floor.

"Grandma Battles, you scared the life out of me. What are you doing over there?"

"Waiting for someone to take me to the mall."

"But it's not even eight," he said putting the pills back into the bottle.

"Old people are on a different time clock."

"What do you need at the mall?"

"A new outfit."

Lex smiled. "I would take you but I'm going to be watching Bert."

"It's all right, Lex. Someone else will be down soon." She pointed to the floor. "You dropped a pill."

"Oh, thanks."

He picked it up, put it onto the kitchen counter, and then looked over at her. Wondering if she could see him, he slowly waved one arm. She didn't respond. He waved both arms. She still didn't respond. He started twisting and turning. Getting no reaction, he stopped.

"You never did have rhythm Lex."

"You can see!"

She got up and walked over to him with her finger up to her lips. "Sssssshhhhh! They'll hear you."

"Did your last eye operation work?"

"No, it didn't."

"But you knew I was twisting and turning."

She laughed. "I also know that you still crush your pills like you did when you were a child."

"Only way I can get them down. So can you see?"

"No Lex. And if I tell you the truth, you won't believe me."

"Try me."

"You see, after I was hit by lightning, which, as you know triggered off my first stroke, that damaged my eyes, she appeared."

"Who did?"

"My little girl. Oh she's a beautiful child with golden curls flowing way down her back."

"Where is she, Grandma?"

"Right now?" She looked up at him. "On your right shoulder."

Lex spun around very quickly and then started to laugh. "Grandma Battles, you're pulling my leg."

"Truly, Lex, I'm not. The doctors call it Charles Bonnet Syndrome but I think God sent her down to help me."

"So what does she do, talk to you?"

"Sometimes. Or she'll guide me so I don't bump into things. Watch."

She walked briskly down the hall as Lex followed her. She entered the dining room, scooted around the table and then returned into the kitchen without bumping into anything.

"Wow, Grandma. Is she always there for you?"

"Probably, Lex. But sometimes I don't listen to her. And when I drink alcohol, she disappears altogether."

"That's incredible."

"She also tells me things." Her voice suddenly turned so sweet and loving. "Like when people are frightened or maybe sick?"

She caught Lex off guard and he immediately started to shake.

"Oh Grandma, I'm so scared."

He embraced her desperately.

"What is it?"

"Cancer."

She grabbed his hands. "Oh, Lex."

"I was going to tell Mother and the rest of you but now that I'm here and seeing Daddy and all, I think it'll be too much."

She reached up and touched his hair. "You can talk to me. I'm a tough cookie."

"Well, there isn't much to say."

"When did you find out?"

"Almost three months ago."

"And how do you feel?"

"Like shit." He poured himself a glass of water and gulped it down. "I had my second cycle of chemotherapy last week, so I'm pretty tired. It's an odd feeling of fatigue. More like being wiped out."

"I guess that makes sense in light of what the drugs are supposed to do."

"Plus it doesn't help that I didn't get a wink of sleep last night."

She picked up the bottle of pills. "What are these for?"

"They keep me from throwing up." He laughed sarcastically. "Well, most of the time."

"Are you doing OK?"

He took the bottle from her, looked at it and then placed it back onto the counter. "It's too soon to tell. What's frustrating is that these drugs make me feel so awful. And of course my hair's falling out. But I also have these weird mouth sores, and food just doesn't taste like food anymore. One part of me says don't do the chemo. It's making you weaker. And some of my friends are pushing me to try alternative methods. But there's a voice inside of me that says to believe in my doctor."

"Then trust that voice, dear. It always knows."

"There's so much more I want to do in life, and yet I feel as though my wings have been clipped."

She walked him to the loveseat in the keeping room and they sat down together. "Me too, darling. But the important thing is that today, now, we're both alive. Right?"

"Right. Peter took me to St. Bart's just before the second cycle, and I had, let's say, the opportunity to check out. I was swimming. You know how I love the water."

"You learned how to swim before you could walk."

"We only went for a long weekend. The day before we came back, the body surfing was fantastic and we both were very happy and in sync."

*   *   *   *

Peter had been worried about Lex, because just recently a close friend of his had committed suicide. Having been diagnosed with an inoperable brain tumor, he opted to kill himself rather than wait for any assortment of horrible scenarios that could have appeared, causing him to die a slow, painful death. And although Lex never talked about ending his own life, Peter knew Lex totally understood and was compassionate about his friend's choice. Peter, on the other hand, was horrified and angered at his decision.

But the vacation Peter treated Lex to was exactly what he had hoped it would be. Rejuvenating for Lex and comforting for himself. In fact, Lex seemed happy and optimistic. He even talked about collaborating on a screenplay with a writing partner in the near future. So it was a surprise to Peter, when at one point, he noticed that Lex had swum really far out into the ocean.

*   *   *   *

"Grandma, I swam farther and farther till I could barely see shore. I felt fish nibbling at my legs. And then my feet got tangled in some seaweed and I stopped swimming. Just like that. I went under. I was choking and swallowing water, but laughing all the time. An almost euphoric feeling came over me and I thought, 'this is it. This is so perfect, I want to go now.' But then I bobbed to the surface and that's when I heard Peter from the shore. He was screaming, 'Lex! Lex please!' His voice was so frightened, it pierced right through me. 'Please come back!' Peter cried desperately. I knew I couldn't leave causing him this much pain, so I swam to shore. I don't know how, but I made it back."

"Oh, Lex." Anastasia held him in her arms. "My heart breaks for you."

"And I couldn't tell the family over the phone. But now that I'm here, I just don't think they'll be able to handle it."

"Don't underestimate the strength of our family. The important thing is, if you tell them now, will it help you?"

"I just don't know."

"Well then, I'll keep your secret, Lex, if you'll keep mine. And maybe God will send you a little guide to help you too."

They were holding onto each other tightly when Bert started to bang the tin cup in his bedroom.

"You OK?" she asked, touching his hair.

"Yup. Thanks, Grandma."

Lex ran to Bert's room as Anastasia got up. She went over to the counter, picked up Lex's pills, hid them in her pocket, and then quickly sat back down in her chair next to the kitchen door.

Like a drill sergeant, Trudy Lee marched down the back stairs into the kitchen and poured herself a cup of coffee. "Mother, not the mall. You'll have to wait. I'm calling a family meeting."

She picked up the phone, dialed, and then looked about her. "Is the Midge up?"

Lex came out of the bedroom with Bert in the rocker, and struggled, sliding him into the bathroom.

"And what about Roscoe?" Trudy Lee spoke into the phone. "Junior, is that you?...Oh, Mattie Lee? What's wrong with your voice? You sound like the Exorcist!...Hello? Hello?..." She turned to Anastasia. "Mattie Lee dropped the phone."

"Who was the last to take a shower?" Mona Lee asked coming down the stairs with her hair wrapped in a towel.

"I was," shouted Lex from the bathroom.

"Well after all that disgusting hair you left in the tub, you ought to be bald." She walked into the kitchen. "Coffee is carcinogenic."

Trudy Lee sipped from her mug. "Good morning to you too, Mona Lee." She shouted into the phone. "Hello? Can anybody hear me?"

Mona Lee poured herself a glass of orange juice as Roscoe came downstairs and prepared himself an Alka-seltzer. They both worked hard at ignoring each other's presence.

Trudy Lee covered the mouthpiece with her hand. "Roscoe? Glad to see you're among the living…Yes, Junior? I want you over here as soon as possible…I know Clairese has you clean the house on Saturday, but this is urgent. You have one minute," she declared as she hung up the phone.

Lex came into the kitchen. "Dad wants his breakfast. Cigarettes and beer." He grabbed them and headed back to the bathroom.

Meanwhile, Trudy Lee raced into the dining room, opened the drawer to the hutch, pulled out a stack of papers, and threw them onto the dining room table. She started rifling through them as quickly as possible.

Exhausted, Lex came out of the bathroom, poured himself a cup of desperately-needed coffee and took it into the dining room. As he sat down next to Trudy Lee, he sneezed.

"Darling, you aren't coming down with something, are you?"

"I hope not."

At that moment, Junior bolted out of the Slaves' Quarters' front door and across the driveway, followed by Clairese and Mattie Lee.

"Junior?" screamed Clairese, already out of breath. "Did you practice the goodbye speech to Bert that I wrote for you? Do you remember the passages I underlined in the Bible that you should recite? Do you think they'll all want me to sing a hymn?" Clairese started humming off key.

"Oh, Lord," mumbled Junior. He dashed up through the screen porch.

"Mattie Lee? I talked to Father Ken. You're going to meet with him this afternoon at three o'clock."

"How long will it take, Mamma?"

"An hour? Two hours? A week? A month? A year?"

"What?"

"As long as it takes for him to be sure you are cleansed, pure and on the right track again." Clairese jumped up onto the porch.

"But Mamma!"

Junior entered Terror's kitchen, screaming. "Is Daddy going?"

"Is he going?" panted Clairese.

"Is he going?" cried Mattie Lee.

"Yeah, he's going to the bathroom," Grandma Battles said from her chair next to the door, as they all ran into the dining room.

Clairese stood there huffing. "This had better be good, Trudy Lee Martindale. Junior was in the middle of vacuuming my ceiling."

"Clairese," whispered Junior, embarrassed.

"Don't Clairese me. I'm sick and tired of your mother calling anytime she pleases. All hours of the day and night. And every time she does, you stop whatever important things you're doing and you come running."

"I don't..."

"That's right, you don't stick up for me and our privacy."

"But..."

"But I have needs, too. And since we are discussing this, I have to admit that at times, I have the feeling that I'm just talking to myself. Thin air!"

"I..."

"I know, I know it's hard to believe and it's probably just my imagination, but I sense that you're tuning me out."

"Clairese?" shouted Trudy Lee. "Either shut up and sit down or take your marital problems elsewhere."

"Full of the devil!" Clairese shrieked, which made Mattie Lee give out a cry.

They all sat around the dining room table, except for Anastasia who was still over by the kitchen door.

"First," continued Trudy Lee, "since some of you think I'm a pathetic, disillusioned little girl, I'm taking charge. There are decisions that have to be made. And we have to make them fast. Junior? You're the accountant. Please go through this clump of papers and tell me where we stand financially." She pushed them towards him. "I know we don't have any money to speak of but…"

"Yes we do," interrupted Mona Lee.

Trudy Lee corrected her. "No we don't. There's our social security and Bert's pension, but that's it."

"But we're upper middle class," Mona Lee said quite snobbishly.

"Try again," shouted Anastasia from the kitchen.

Mona Lee looked at each one of them for agreement. "But I thought Daddy made lots of money."

"Credit, my dear," Trudy Lee said. "We've always lived on credit. Junior, see if you can find your father's life insurance policy. Lex, you're the writer. The obituaries are your responsibility. I want him in all the local papers. I've written up a bio that you can work from." She handed him a paper. "Your father wants to be cremated."

"Mother," whispered Mona Lee. "He's sitting in the bathroom."

"Get over it, Mona Lee."

"How can you be so flip? I'll never get over my father's death. Never!"

She buried her head in her hands as Trudy Lee looked over at Lex with an evil smile. Picking up on her intense desire at that moment to tell her daughter who her real father was, Lex smiled and shook his head no.

"As I was saying," Trudy Lee continued, "I have no idea how much a cremation costs."

"Cremation alone, $1,500.00, bottom line," Lex said casually.

"That's outrageous," cried Clairese.

"Extra for putting the ashes into a receptacle," added Lex.

Everyone in the room looked at him, wondering where and

why he would know this information.

"Ah, well, I was curious one day so I went into a funeral home and asked them how much a cremation costs."

Trudy Lee carried on. "Anyway, so what do we do with his ashes?"

"Throw them out to sea, off the pier at Cape Hatteras," suggested Mona Lee. "That was his favorite place."

Trudy Lee sneered. "And with our luck a wind will come along and he'll blow back in our faces."

"Should we have a funeral?" asked Roscoe.

"He's an atheist," declared Lex.

"How about a memorial?" suggested Junior.

Trudy Lee put up her hand. "Wait. Let's get back to what we're going to do with his ashes."

Anastasia appeared in the dining room doorway. "Why don't you put him out back with Bob?"

They all gave her a dirty look.

"West Parish will take him," sniffled Mattie Lee. "They'll take anyone. They're Lesbyterian."

Clairese corrected her. "That's Presbyterian."

"I like West Parish," admitted Roscoe.

"Me, too," said Lex. "It's so pretty."

"And they have that beautiful gate leading into the cemetery," smiled Trudy Lee.

"And the way those walkways just sweep through and around those big old oak trees," sighed Mona Lee.

"And it looks like there's plenty of room," added Junior.

There was a period of silence and Grandma Battles chimed in with, "Gee, why don't we all go. We'll have them line our tombstones up in a semi-circle. Like a big smile face."

The room was silent a moment longer and then they all broke out into laughter.

"See," exclaimed Trudy Lee. "This is good. We're all together as a family and laughing. Laughing real hard."

"Mother?" Junior interrupted while shuffling the papers. "I don't think you'll find this funny."

"What is it?" she asked.

"Father's at least twenty thousand-dollars in debt and…"

"And what?"

"And he's borrowed on his life insurance policies. You may have to declare bankruptcy."

"I'm going to kill him," growled Trudy Lee.

NINE

I'M SINNING AND IT FEELS SO GOOD

Later that morning, Trudy Lee sped down Route 1 headed toward the mall in her van. She was wearing a gigantic, broadbrimmed hat, huge sunglasses, pearls, gloves and a cocktail dress. In the passenger seat, and just barely able to see over the dash, was Mona Lee. In the back seat were Grandma Battles, Mattie Lee, and Clairese.

Trudy Lee adjusted her hat so she could partially see while she rode on the heels of the driver in front of her.

Instinctively, Mona Lee pushed her right foot into the floorboards, trying to slow the car down. "Mother, stop tailgating."

"I'm not. That crazy driver's going too slow. I can't see." She looked into the rear view mirror and checked her make-up. "Can I change lanes?"

Mattie Lee peered out the window as Trudy Lee hit the gas hard. "No."

Trudy Lee changed lanes as tires from the car beside them screeched. She swerved back, and everyone in the van was thrown, as the other driver leaned on the horn.

The van sped down the highway, weaving recklessly from lane to lane. Once at the mall, it was the expected and dreaded parking scenario.

Mona Lee pointed to the right. "You just passed a spot."

Trudy Lee shook her hat. "It's too far away."

She sped the van up to the front of the mall and drove down the parking lot looking for spots one more time.

"There!" screamed Clairese. "Back one space."

Trudy Lee was determined. "I can find one closer." She made a frighteningly sharp right turn and raced to the front of the mall, again.

Mattie Lee looked to her left. "There was one back…"

Trudy Lee swerved the car violently and screeched the brakes. She tried to squeeze into a spot that was too small for the van, as Clairese rubbed her fogged-up window with the sleeve of her coat. "You can't park here, Trudy Lee."

Mona Lee squinted to read the sign. "It's for the physically challenged."

"We're all handicapped," Trudy Lee whispered as she jerked the car forward and swiped the car next to them. The van was parked at a severe angle.

*　*　*　*

Back at Terror, Lex was on his hands and knees, scrubbing the kitchen floor, when Roscoe came running down the back stairs with his golf clubs.

"Lex?" he asked looking into the keeping room.

"I'm in the kitchen, Rosc."

He walked in. "Where?"

Lex popped his head up over the counter. "Down here. Something is cemented to this kitchen floor."

Roscoe looked nervously out the kitchen window. "Is the coast clear?"

"Mona Lee's at the mall looking for crystals."

"Lex, can I talk to you?" Roscoe was really anxious.

Lex stood up and emptied his pail of water while Roscoe looked down the front hall, and then out through the screen porch door, to see if anyone was coming. He ran to Bert's door, which was ajar, looked in quickly and then closed it, running back to Lex.

"I promise this will only take a minute."

"What's up?" Lex asked.

"I'm leaving."

"To play golf?"

"No. To Alaska."

"You're going back to Alaska? Roscoe, do you think bartending is the best profession for you?"

"No. My best friend Rick? His brother works a fishing boat off of Kodiak Island. He's the best deck hand in Alaska. He's twenty-five, been doing it for seven years, and he makes hundreds of thousands of dollars a year."

Lex took a deep breath and started washing his hands. "Well, what would you do?"

"Halibut are running early this year. The government opens up twenty-four hour windows, allowing fishermen to catch as many fish as they can in that time period."

"So you'll be fishing in a boat in the Pacific for twenty-four hours?"

"Well, actually, I'll be down below, gutting the fish and stuffing their bellies full of ice."

Lex just couldn't believe that Roscoe was going off on another wild goose chase for imaginary money. "Gosh, it sounds like hard work."

"It is, Lex. But like I said, I could make easily close to a million my first season. I'm going to wait till..." he whispered, "...Dad is gone, and then I'm off."

"Gee Rosc. I was hoping you and I could spend more time together. It seems as though we've grown so far apart these last few years."

"Why?"

"Because I…"

"Lex, give it up. You and I were never close." His honesty hit Lex to the core. "I just have to get away from this family. This house."

There was an awkward silence.

"But what about golfing? Are you just going to give it up?"

"Yeah. It's about time I started getting realistic about my life." Lex smiled as Roscoe continued. "Let's face it. I wasn't making any money at it. So I'm going to run down to the pro shop at the golf course and see if I can sell my clubs."

"I guess you gotta do what you gotta do."

"Yeah. Don't say anything to Mother or anybody. Not yet."

Lex wanted to throw his arms around his little brother, but being a true Martindale he just opted to stand there. "No. No I won't."

"OK. Well, I guess I better get down to the course."

Roscoe ran out the screen porch door followed by Lex.

"Good luck, Roscoe," Lex whispered to himself, as he watched him wobble off on his bicycle.

*　*　*　*

Mona Lee, wearing red and orange polka-dot balloon pants and a bright lemon satin blouse, slumped up against the make-up counter at Your Best Face Forward cosmetics store.

"Mother!" shouted Mona Lee.

"I can't talk," mumbled Trudy Lee as she sat with her back to Mona Lee. "I'm having my lips lined."

Mona Lee picked up a bottle of foundation and read the ingredients. "I hope these cosmetics weren't tested on any animals."

"Oh no," reassured Carmela the beautician. "We don't have any cosmetics for animals. These are only for human use."

Mona Lee couldn't believe how stupid she was.

"Do you think I'll be able to do this myself at home, Carmela?" Trudy Lee asked.

"Of course. See, I've worked from stencils." She held one up in the shape of lips. "Just tape it on and fill in the blanks. I have them for eyebrows too."

"How remarkable," exclaimed Trudy Lee as Carmela spun her around.

"Oh my God," screamed Mona Lee.

"What? What?" asked Trudy Lee as she looked in the mirror.

"For God's sake, Mother. You look like Mrs. Potato Head."

"Mona Lee, that's a terrible thing to say about Carmela's artistry. She graduated from the Wanton Bluff School of Beauty."

"I'm a trained cosmetologist," Carmela said proudly.

"For what? Funeral parlors? It looks like she's wearing a pair of wax lips."

"Mona Lee," her mother said disgusted with her, "we're all meeting at Bras! Bras! Bras! at 2:30. So why don't you go off and buy yourself those gerbils you wanted."

"Gerbils Mother?"

Trudy Lee shooed her away with her hands. "That wheat gerbil mix you like to eat."

"Ugh. That's wheat germ," She picked up her bags as she rolled her eyes. "I'm out of here. Just being in this mall is making me sick. I'll find my own way home."

"Suit yourself." Trudy Lee turned back to Carmela as Mona Lee clumped off.

"Trudy Lee, do you trust me?" asked Carmela.

"Explicitly."

Carmela smiled and rubbed her hands together in excitement. "Fat, plump, luscious lips are in. We've just used lip stencil number one. How about we do it again, with stencil number three? That will extend your lips out another quarter of an inch?"

"I'm game," Trudy Lee smiled.

Mona Lee turned left out of Your Best Face Forward and noticed the bookstore across the walkway. In the front window was a tower of books. On closer inspection she was able to read the cover of the book.

"*Marital Monogamy* by Professor Bobby Mack Beerbower," Mona Lee read out loud. "That fucker wrote a book?"

And there on the front of every cover was Professor Bobby Mack Beerbower's smug little mug.

"The goddamn stinking mother fucker wrote a book about monogamy?" Mona Lee exclaimed much louder this time.

A young boy passing by turned to his mother and asked, "What's a mother fucker?" The mother dragged him away from Mona Lee as she seethed in front of the store window.

Blinded with rage, Mona Lee did not see Professor Bobby Mack Beerbower seated at the book signing table just inside the store. And because no one was asking him to sign his books, he was blankly staring out the window when he saw Mona Lee. Eventually, she saw him waving to her.

"Shit!" she screamed as she darted away from the window.

Bobby Mack got up from the table and walked out into the mall. "Mona Lee?" he called out, but she was nowhere to be found.

Next to the bookstore was a pretzel cart. And crouching down behind the pretzel cart was Mona Lee, hiding.

"Mona Lee Martindale?" called out Professor Bobby Mack Beerbower again.

She held her breath and broke out into a sweat as her thoughts rushed back to the fall of 1969.

* * * *

A freshman at the North Carolina Community College for Arts and Sciences, Mona Lee was fresh and looking for a man. This peach was so ripe she was ready to fall off the tree.

Granted, in high school she was always surrounded by a bevy of boys, but she never had a boyfriend. Everyone, including her family, questioned her sexuality. In fact, Trudy Lee always thought she'd make a brilliant lesbian. But the truth was, she just hadn't met the right guy. Mona Lee wasn't interested in school-boy crushes. Now that doesn't mean, like all the other Martindale women, she wasn't incredibly sexual and flirtatious. She was, but she didn't act upon it. She was holding out for true love. Hence, she entered college a bona fide virgin of both body and soul.

NCCC sat on the far western border of North Carolina; there-fore it was necessary for her to live on campus. It was a coed school and she was placed in a coed dorm. And she lucked out and got a room to herself.

As a child, Mona Lee was extremely athletic. A tomboy, who was lean and strong, she could outrun anybody her age. For that matter, she could outrun just about anyone, period. This was one thing that brought her very close to Bert. And it delighted him to no end to find out that his daughter had signed up for track and field in her freshman year of college.

She had just turned nineteen and weighed only ninety pounds. She had long brown hair that came halfway down her back, and like her mother, she had great legs and wasn't afraid to show them off. Mini-skirts were still popular and she loved wearing them. And, although not necessarily pretty, she had a very attrac-tive, sexy, earthiness about her.

Not sure what she wanted to major in, Mona Lee signed up for liberal arts. And a mandatory class she had to take was Psych 101. But when she put on her crisp, white button-down shirt, tar-tan micro pleated skirt, white knee socks with penny loafers, and walked into the first day of that class, she took one look at her teacher and knew her major was going to be Professor Bobby Mack Beerbower.

More interested in running the 440-yard dash than hitting the books, Mona Lee struggled with psychology. Hence, it made all the sense in the world to her that she should sign up for private study classes offered by Professor Beerbower.

Back in 1969 Bobby Mack was cute and he knew it. He looked as though he had stepped right out of central casting. He had smoky gray eyes, and although he was only twenty-four years old, he was already developing white hair about the temples, which was a total turn-on for Mona Lee. And he wore tweed jackets with leather elbow patches, khaki pants, loafers and even smoked a pipe. Mona Lee pegged him as a total cliché, but she was hooked.

When she had private tutorials with him, she'd sit close enough to smell his body. He had a clean, fresh laundry smell about him, mixed with spicy pipe tobacco. And his teeth were absolutely perfect and white.

And it was clear to the professor that Mona Lee was more interested in him than in Psych 101.

"But what does subliminal mean, Professor Beerbower?" she asked knowing very well what it meant.

"Well, ah...," he cleared his throat. "Subliminal means below the threshold of consciousness."

"But we're both conscious, right?" she asked softly.

"Yes, yes. We are definitely conscious."

She brought her lips close to his ear and asked, "Would subliminal mean...subtle?"

"No, no, you're not subtle...at all. I mean subliminal is ah, more, more than subtle."

"There's a track meet Thursday afternoon," Mona Lee whispered.

"Thursday afternoon, you say?"

"Three o'clock. I'd like you to come watch me."

"Oh, would you?"

She put her hand on top of his thigh. "I run the 440. And I'm fast."

He coughed nervously. "I can tell you are. Ah, I mean, I'm sure you are."

Having made her first pass at Professor Bobby Mack Beer-bower, Mona Lee took off in the lead. And what a race it was.

It was the first meet of the season and Bert drove across from Ragland to cheer Mona Lee on. The sun was bright and the air was crisp, hinting that fall weather was on its way. And even though Mona Lee loved running, organized competition made her nauseous. Really nauseous. So much so that she vomited just before her race began.

There were five women competing, each having her own lane. Mona Lee was given number one. She wore her school track uniform, a tank top and a rather skimpy, stretchy, brief pair of shorts. She looked tiny compared to the other runners, but strong.

"On your marks," hollered the starter.

When Mona Lee took her mark, she quickly glanced into the bleachers and saw Bert, who gave her the thumbs up. And then she noticed Bobby Mack sitting in the row just behind him and to his left. He smiled at her. It was then that she realized how much he looked like Bert. As a matter of fact, anyone sitting in the stands glancing over at them would have wondered if they were father and son. She smiled back, trying not to vomit again and focused on the race.

"Get set...Go!" yelled the official as he fired his gun. At first, because it was a staggered start and she was in the inside lane, Mona Lee seemed to be way in the back. The race was once around the track and because her legs were so short, she looked as though she were running twice as fast as everyone else. By the time she had made it up to the 220 mark it was clear she was out in the lead.

Bert jumped to his feet, and with so much pride and enthusiasm screamed, "That's it girl! Go girl! You go Mona Lee!"

Everybody in the bleachers stood up and cheered her on as she came around the last quarter. But one runner from the other team was inching up on Mona Lee, so Bert screamed louder.

"Open up your stride! Relax and open it up, Mona Lee!"

The other girl started to pass Mona Lee, who now felt as though she was going to pass out. Her mouth was dry, her stomach sick and her legs felt heavy and thick.

And that's when Bobby Mack hollered out, "Run, Mona Lee! No time to be subtle! Run, Mona Lee! Run like the wind!"

She heard him. She felt him. And with that added burst of support, she suddenly got her second wind and breezed by her competitor, and won the race by only a stride.

Everyone went crazy. The coach and teammates ran to Mona Lee and picked her up. Bert jumped up and down in the bleachers. Bobby Mack even tapped him on the shoulder and shook his hand, introducing himself.

And later that evening, after she had had dinner with Bert and he had left to drive back to Ragland, Mona Lee had a planned rendezvous with Professor Bobby Mack Beerbower in her dorm room. She knew practically nothing about him except that she wanted him. And he felt the same way. So, on that victorious day in October of 1969, Mona Lee won the race of her life and then lost her virginity.

As a lover, Bobby Mack was everything she'd dreamed of. He was sensitive, caring, generous, attentive and hungry. Mona Lee had fallen madly in love, and the two of them continued to see each other secretly several times a week through the rest of that school semester and into the spring.

But it was during one particular late afternoon get-together that they had in her dorm room, just before Easter, when Mona Lee had to ask Bobby about something that was upsetting her.

They had just made love and were still under the sheets when she asked him point blank, "Why don't we ever go out?"

He laughed a bit nervously and put his hands behind his head on the pillow. "Mona Lee, we go out. I see you in class. The cafeteria. The library."

She propped herself up on her elbow and looked him in the

eye. "No. We don't go out on dates. We never go to the movies. We've never been out to dinner. Don't you want to be seen with me?"

"Well, sure I want to be seen with you. We'll go out. We'll go out, soon. I promise. It's just so much…nicer…sexier…intimate …to be here."

He kissed her and started making love to her again, but she didn't buy it. She sensed something was wrong. He was pulling away from her. Deep down, she felt panic. This was virgin territory for her, no pun intended, and she didn't know what to do. After he left her room that day, she felt that same nauseous feeling that bubbled up in her gut whenever she was about to run a race.

Having devoted all of her free time to Bobby Mack, Mona Lee had absolutely no friends at school. No one to turn to when she realized, a week later, she was late for her period. She had gotten birth control pills from the school infirmary, but she wasn't strict about taking them. And since the onset of menstruation, her periods had always appeared like clockwork.

She wanted to run and tell Bobby Mack what she suspected, but with his being a bit distant she was afraid this might wedge a bigger gap between them. So she waited till the time was perfect to tell him the good news.

It was lunch the following week and she still had not had her period.

"Bobby Mack, there's something I need to tell you."

"Mona Lee, I have to say something too. Something that I've been wanting to say for a long time."

She was totally thrown. "Oh?"

He touched her hand. "But you go first."

"No, I'll wait. What is it?"

"Geez Mona Lee, I was practicing how to say this all the way over here and now I just don't know…"

Thrilled that he was about to pop the question she gasped,

"Just say it, Bobby Mack. Trust me, I'm a big girl."

"Well, I know I should have told you right away, but..."

"But what?"

"But...I'm married."

Mona Lee was stunned.

"I know. I know. I...I...should have told you right up front but...you see...my wife and I..."

She pulled her hand away from his and looked at it. "You don't wear a wedding band."

"No. No I don't and that's because of what I was just going to say. That she and I, well, we've had our problems and we've talked about splitting up and well...it seems as though she's... well, we're going to have a baby."

Mona Lee could not believe what she was hearing. "You've been having sex with her...while you've been making love to me?"

"Uh...well...yes...it appears so," he said rather guiltily. She was speechless as he continued. "And well...we don't want to get an abortion. Well, she doesn't and I would never force her to, so we are going to try to work on our relationship and even maybe go into some therapy and bring the baby into this world with two...happy parents and..."

With that, Mona Lee got up from the table, ran to the ladies room and threw up.

The next day, by herself, she went to an abortion clinic just off campus and got rid of the fetus. She called a cab after the procedure and spent the next few days holed up in her dorm room. But unfortunately, an infection set in. Instead of going back to the clinic right away, Mona Lee waited it out. Almost a week later, with a temperature of a hundred and four, she passed out on the dorm's bathroom floor and was then rushed to the hospital. She made one phone call to one person.

Bert stood outside of Mona Lee's room with a nurse who was shaking her head. "If only she had come in at the first signs of infection after the abortion."

Without Mona Lee's seeing him, Bert looked through the door at her. The nurse touched his arm.

"It was abscessed and beyond repair. We had to give her a hysterectomy."

Bert entered Mona Lee's room and stood by her bed. She sensed who was standing there and embarrassed, turned her head to him.

"Please don't tell anyone. Especially Mother. I'm sorry Daddy."

Exhausted, Mona Lee fell asleep, as Bert's eyes teared up.

When she was strong enough, she left college before completing that first year. And no one in the family knew what had happened to Mona Lee and why she mysteriously returned home. No one knew that she had fallen head-over-heels for her psychology professor. No one knew that she had an endured an abortion and the medical incident had left her sterile.

The dreadful ordeal crushed something deep inside of Bert. Emotionally, losing his little girl to this awful tragedy felt as devastating to him as when he had lost his own mother. Maybe if he had been a more evolved man he could have worked through it and helped to heal his daughter and himself. But his relationship with Mona Lee was never the same again. And sadly, they gradually drifted farther and farther apart.

* * * *

And Mona Lee never saw Professor Bobby Mack Beerbower again until that very day.

"Mona Lee?" he hollered once more, looking about the mall.

He finally came around the pretzel stand and saw her crunched down near the floor.

"Mona Lee?"

She hid her face with her hand. "No. No, my name is not Mona

148

Lee. Ah, I dropped something."

He reached out for her hand and helped her up.

"I'm sorry. You look like an old friend of mine."

Mona Lee wouldn't look him in the eye as he held onto her.

"No." Flustered, embarrassed, cornered and angry, she blurted out, "I have no friends. Please leave me alone."

She pulled her hand away from his and ran down the mall right past Clairese who was looking for Mattie Lee and Anastasia.

"Mona Lee?" she hollered.

"No, I'm not Mona Lee," she yelled back.

"What?" Clairese stood there asking herself.

Mona Lee ran to the far end of the mall and ducked around a corner to catch her breath. Flashbacks of college, Bobby Mack and their days of making love flooded her brain, as tears streamed down her face. Even though it had taken place over twenty years ago, the pain was still so raw for her that it all felt as though it had happened yesterday.

"*Marital Monogamy*," Mona Lee cried to herself. "You bastard."

Meanwhile, Clairese continued searching the mall for her daughter.

"Mattie Lee? Grandma Battles?" She walked into a music store. "Grandma Battles? Mattie Lee?"

Across the way, Mattie Lee darted back into a dress shop. "We've ditched her, Grandma."

"Good," she shouted from the changing room. "I'm coming out Mattie Lee."

She emerged wearing a day-glow orange pantsuit. "How do I look?"

"Bright."

"Good. Men respond to bright colors."

Suddenly, Mattie Lee started to cry.

"Oh dear, do I look that bad?"

"No Grandma, you look great," she cried harder.

She sat down next to Mattie Lee. "Then what is it? What's the matter?"

"Men!" she screamed.

"I know. I know. Boyfriend troubles?"

"Worse!"

"Girlfriend troubles?"

"No." Mattie Lee struggled to find the words. "Grandma... you're the only one I feel comfortable and safe talking to about this."

"Yes?"

"I have baby troubles."

"I don't follow."

"Grandma Battles, I'm pregnant!" Mattie Lee shouted. The saleswoman and two customers looked at her with horror.

There was a moment and then Anastasia burst out into laughter. "You're such a prankster, Mattie Lee."

"No, I'm serious. Lowell Lovejoy made me pregnant."

"Which one is Lowell?"

"The dopey seven-year-old."

Anastasia held back her snicker, knowing Mattie Lee was dead serious.

"And now my mamma and daddy know, and Father Ken, I think, is giving me an abortion at three o'clock."

Grandma Battles put her hand in Mattie Lee's. "Dear, you just turned ten, right?"

"Yes."

"And do you already have the curse?"

"My mamma says I'm possessed and full of the devil."

"Well, she says that about everyone. No darling, what I mean is, have you been visited by your friend yet?"

Mattie Lee thought about it. "No. No friend has visited me, well, except Lowell that is, but I don't really call him a friend."

"And what makes you think you're pregnant?"

Mattie Lee whispered under her breath. "Because if a woman has an egg and the man has the germs, pow, you're pregnant."

Grandma Battles couldn't hold back the laughter any longer. "Oh my dear, you've got it all wrong. Is this the way your mother explained the birds and the bees to you?"

"She hasn't explained anything."

"That figures. What do you say, we get these dresses for me and then I'll buy you an ice cream and explain the facts of life to you. And Mattie Lee?"

"Yes, Grandma Battles?"

"You are not pregnant."

"I'm not?"

"I promise."

She gave her great grandmother a huge hug. "Oh thank you."

"But I wonder what your mother has planned for you with Father Ken?"

Mattie Lee scratched under her sweatshirt. "This is itching me so much."

"What is?"

Mattie Lee pulled out her Bible workbook. "My mamma tied this around my neck." She pulled it off, up over her head.

"Why in God's name do you have a Bible workbook tied around your neck?"

"I've stopped trying to figure my mother out."

Anastasia flipped through it. "And what is a Bible notebook?"

"You study a book of the Bible and then answer questions. I know all the answers but I filled in phony ones cause I get bored in class."

"Mmmm. This is getting very interesting. Read one of your favorites to me."

"You sure?"

"Yeah, hit me with a good one."

Mattie Lee flipped open her book. "You asked for it. The last question for this week's lesson was: Please name the Holy Trinity."

Grandma Battles prepared herself. "And the answer is...?"

"The Father, the Son and the Holy shit."

"That's my girl," cackled Anastasia as she slapped her knee. "You're a true Martindale."

Back at Terror, Lex had just finished cleaning the kitchen and was starting in on Bert's bathroom when the phone rang. He answered the kitchen extension in a very forced, deep voice.

"Helloooo?"

"Hello?" asked the person hesitantly. "Mrs. Martindale?"

Lex almost dropped the phone. "Peter, it's me."

He laughed. "Why did you answer the phone like that?"

Lex nervously walked around the kitchen. "Because, when I was a kid, everyone thought I was either my mother or Mona Lee or some other woman."

"I guess we still do."

"Ha ha."

Peter turned genuine. "How's it going?"

Lex took a deep breath. "Thank God you didn't come. Madness. Sheer madness."

"What's wrong?"

He reached into a cupboard and took out the Alka-seltzer. "Well, I'm already shaking and throwing up."

"You threw up?"

Lex took down a drinking glass and was just about to fill it with water when he noticed how dirty it was. "Yeah, on my birthday pie. How are you? What's up?"

"Your agent called. I didn't tell her to call you, not knowing what was going on. There's an editor that has seen the dummy children's book, likes it, but wants revisions done yesterday, and then she'll consider taking it on."

"Which publishing house is it?"

"Galaxias?"

"Why the rush?"

"You tell me."

"What does Betty think?"

"Considering no one else is biting, she says, 'go for it.'"

Frustrated, Lex put the glass down. "I don't know if I can leave. My father's..." Lex walked towards Bert's room and continued whispering, "It's really awful." He turned around and started washing the glass at the sink.

Junior stuck his head in through the screen porch door, saw Lex and walked in very tentatively. The phone conversation continued without Lex's knowing he was there.

Peter paused and then asked the big question. "Have you told your family?"

"I talked to Grandma."

"How did you tell her?"

Lex started washing the glass harder. "She knew."

"What?"

"Peter, it's a long story and Mattie Lee senses something's off. Isn't that interesting? The youngest and the oldest?"

"But you have to tell your mother."

"I know!" Lex snapped back and suddenly the glass broke in his hand. "Shoot!"

"What just happened?"

Lex grabbed paper towels and shoved them into the palm of his hand. "Nothing. I'm going to tell Trudy Lee. It's just that I haven't found the right moment."

There was a pause. "How do you feel?"

"Like a toxic waste dump. Ooooohhhhh! Fudge! God! I can't even swear in this house," he laughed. "Why is it that every time I come home, I regress back to the role of a twelve-year-old referee?"

Junior coughed to get Lex's attention. Startled, he spun around.

"Junior just walked in."

Peter took his cue. "I'll let you go."

"OK. I'll call back in a short while."

"I miss you."

Without responding, Lex hung up the phone. "Hey Junior."

"Are you all right? I mean I hope you don't think I was eaves-dropping?"

"You know me and my allergies. They seem to be flaring up again."

"Oh, well, if that's all," Junior replied sensing it was much more than that. "Did you cut yourself?"

Lex looked at his palm. "Just a scratch."

There was a long pause as Lex washed his hands.

"Lex? With everyone at the mall I thought it would give us a chance to catch up on things."

"Great, let's talk."

There was a pause as Junior stared at him, saying nothing. Uncomfortable with the silence, Lex picked up the broken glass, threw it into the trash and started babbling. "That was Peter. Another publishing house seems to be interested in the book. I may have to fly back to New York. By the way, it's not on the bestseller list and I had a talk with Mother about her stretching the truth and all."

"That's good. That's good."

There was another painful pause, so Lex continued. "Pete phoned to say our agent had called."

Junior smiled a little too hard. "I hope some day soon I'll get to meet him. He sounds like a nice guy."

"He is. You and Mattie Lee and Clairese should come up for a visit."

Unexpectedly, Junior burst into tears.

"Junior?" He cried harder and Lex went to his side. "Junior? What is it? It's Dad. Yes. We're all upset. Just let it out."

Junior shook his head.

He was about to place his palm on Junior's back, saw the blood and switched to the other hand. He tried to touch him but it just hovered. "It's not Dad?"

He nodded his head.

"It is Dad but something else too?"

He sobbed louder.

"Junior? Please. Talk to me? Are you having problems at work? Are you sick? Is it Clairese?"

Junior wailed.

"Well, what's wrong?"

"I can't get a word in edgewise, Lex."

"I'm sorry. Go ahead."

"No, I mean with Clairese. She never stops talking."

Lex went back to the sink. "Well, I have noticed that when you're together you don't seem to say much."

"It must sound so...petty." He broke down crying again.

Lex grabbed another glass and filled it with water. "No, not at all."

"It's gotten so bad, I've been seeing a therapist."

Lex dropped the Alka-seltzer into the water and watched it fiz. "Shouldn't Clairese be the one?"

"We've talked about it. Well, she's talked about it, but she thinks I'm the one with the problem."

"Gee, Junior. Well, is the therapist helping?"

"Yes, we're having sex now."

"You and Clairese." Lex started to drink the antacid.

"No, me and the therapist."

Lex choked and cleared his throat. "Is that legal?"

"Oh my God. Lex. I'm committing adultery. I'm sinning and it feels so good." He started crying again. "Oh I love Clairese...kind of...and she's a good person...kind of...and she's always there for Mattie Lee...kind of...but she never listens to me."

"Well what happens when you do start to talk?"

"She cuts me off, and whatever I'm talking about, she relates it to herself, and then she just talks at me, kind of. Even in bed, she never stops and it just makes my talliwacker shrivel all up, real small. It's so frustrating."

"I can imagine."

"And my therapist, oh, did I tell you she's a woman?"

Lex shook his head.

"Yeah, well, I mean I don't have anything against people of the same sex doing it and all. I mean there's you and your Peter and well that's OK if that's what you prefer and all."

There was a moment of silence and then the two brothers shared a hearty chuckle.

"Yes, Junior, I know it's OK."

"It's just that my therapist, she sits there in her office in this big Naugahyde chair and I start talking and she listens. She listens so hard and she's sitting in that chair and I get so excited and before I know it, I've got my clothes off. And we're going at it, right there in her office. And she's the best, Lex. She's the best I've ever had."

"But how long can you keep it up?"

"Well, a session lasts about an hour."

"No, I mean this charade."

"I don't know Lex. She's expensive. I'm running out of money."

Just then, Mona Lee came in through the screen porch in her ridiculous outfit.

"Back so soon?" Lex asked.

"It's too embarrassing for me to be seen in public with our family. I took a cab home. All of them. They're so weird. Mother is going to every make-up counter having her face done over. She looks like a whore. And I don't get Grandma Battles. After eighty-five years of wearing muumuus, and now, after going blind, she has to become a fashion statement? She's trying everything on in every store. Mattie Lee is moping around and crying every time someone speaks to her, and that Clairese? Junior, I don't know how you put up with her. She's always had diarrhea mouth, but I swear she's getting worse. Talk, talk, talk, talk, talk, talk, talk, talk!"

Junior looked at his watch. "I forgot I've got a doctor's appointment." He bolted out of the house.

"He's weird too," Mona Lee declared.

Junior jumped into his car, roared the engine and took off. "One, two, three, four, five, six, seven beating fists," he happily screamed as he raced down the driveway.

He pulled out onto River Road without looking, and just missed another car. "Howdy Neighbor," he laughed as he took a left and zoomed off to his appointment.

His therapist's office was in a small strip mall just across Shawsheen River, and over the railroad tracks in Ballardvale.

Junior sped into the parking lot and parked his car on an illegal angle. He jumped out and ran along the mall. Past the Shawsheen Drycleaners, past the Knit One, Pearl Too craft store, past Dunfee's Sub Shop to the last establishment on the strip. He stood in front of her office and touched her sign. It read: *Dr. Belle Pepper, Esoteric Counselor at Large.*

* * * *

Dr. Belle Pepper mysteriously appeared in Ragland in the early 1960s. And, because at one time or another she quietly serviced just about every straight man in town, she was allowed to continue her rather unorthodox therapy practice, illegally. No one was quite sure who she was or where she had come from. But if they had taken the time and effort and done their homework, they would have discovered that Dr. Belle Pepper was none other than Ragland's very own Florence Shlotz.

She grew up on a dairy farm that her mother had inherited from her parents, in a town south of Ragland called Rolling Ridge. As a teenager she was a homely girl with eyeglasses, mousy brown hair, pimples, discolored teeth from taking antibiotics as a young child, and no breasts to speak of. Florence was not a popular girl. In fact, she had no friends at all. And when she wasn't buried in a book that was whisking her off to some faraway romantic place, she was attending to her pet pig, Tulip. In fact, the summer before her senior year of high school, Florence, being a member of her local 4-H Club, entered Tulip into the bovine competition at the Monmouth North Carolina County Fair.

It was Labor Day weekend when the final day of judging occurred and Florence's mother, father and sister, April, watched on as she won first in show and was crowned *Miss Bovine Of Tomorrow.*

To celebrate, Florence and her family played the carnival games, watched other 4-H competitions and rode just about every amusement park ride at the fair.

Prone to motion sickness, Florence decided to pass on subjecting herself to the last and final ride…the Mammoth Monmouth Monster Mobile. On the outside of this circular contraption, painted on plywood cutouts, were caricatures of classic monsters like the Mummy, Frankenstein and the Werewolf. People would stand upright facing the center and centrifugal force would hold them in place as the ride spun them around and then tilted on its side.

And while she was sharing her third ball of purple cotton candy with Tulip, and getting mildly sick trying to focus on her family as they blurrily spun around, the Mammoth Monmouth Monster Mobile unfortunately unhinged from its base and tore through the County Fair, killing not only all on board, but everyone in its path as well.

The coroner's and investigative reports concluded that it was a freak and tragic accident. But the truth was that Florence's father was a chronic gambler. Far more interested in betting on horses than milking cows, Harold Shlotz was addicted to the racetrack. Alas, he was way over his head in debt, and one-too-many times too late in paying back his bookie, who was an intern working for North Carolina's one and only Mafia family, the Rogusto brothers.

As fate would have it, the Rogustos owned every carnie booth, side show and amusement ride at the County Fair. And infuriated by Harold Shlotz's nonchalant attitude towards honoring his debts, the Rogusto brothers cleverly rigged the Mammoth Monmouth Monster Mobile so that it would look like it had naturally torn away from its foundation. What looked like the County's worst accident was, in truth, its most hideous murder.

The Shlotz's farm was sold to pay off debts, and seventeen-year-old shell-shocked Florence and her award-winning pig, Tulip, were begrudgingly sent off by authorities to live with her mother's sister, whose name was, ironically, Titti.

Florence, upon arriving at the Ragland home of her very poor and prudish Aunt Titti's, was not a happy girl. And adding insult to injury, she was horrified when Aunt Titti promptly had Tulip butchered, quartered and frozen, ready for dinner, each and every Sunday after Church. Florence became a vegetarian and an atheist.

On top of that, she had to adjust to entering a new high school in her senior year. Again, with no friends to speak of and never having fitted in, Florence was desperate for the teasing and taunting from schoolmates to end, and therefore was eager to jump into the adult world upon graduation in 1953.

She applied for a civil service job and ended up as a secretary, working for none other than Peyton Pomp. And although Peyton was overweight, bald and was two inches shorter than Florence, she immediately fell madly in love with him.

For the next three years she worked hard for, and pined even harder over, Peyton Pomp. But it was an unrequited love. Peyton definitely acknowledged Florence's secretarial skills, especially her ability to shred without questions. But never, not once, did he notice or think of Florence in a romantic kind of way.

And the day he jumped ship and jumped onto a ship for Belize, Florence had to tell him what she felt in her heart.

"But let me come with you," pleaded Florence as Peyton scurried around the office grabbing important and/or incriminating documents.

"Why?" he asked dryly, as he tried to shoo her off.

"Because...because...because I..."

"Because you what?" he asked annoyed.

"I said...said...I said," she stuttered as he pushed her out of the way while reaching for his American Tobacco Company honorary plaque.

"You know I'm in a rush, Hortance," he shouted.

"Florence."

"What?" he asked.

"My name is Florence, not Hortance," she said, rather deflated.

"Sure, kid." He spun around, throwing the last things into a box, and proceeded to the door.

"Stop," ordered Florence raising her voice. Peyton stood still and then turned around. With every ounce of courage in her she blurted out, "Take me with you."

He paused for a moment, surprised at her moxie. "And why would I do that?"

"Because...because...I love you, Peyton."

There was a moment of total silence as Florence searched his blank face for some sort of response.

"You what me?" he asked quietly.

"I love you," she confessed sensitively. "I've loved you since the first day we met."

Peyton Pomp looked at her and then burst into laughter. "That is the funniest thing I have ever heard."

"What?" she asked stunned.

"You and me?" he continued. "Sweetheart, you're a great secretary, but in the looks department, I'd date a toothless hooker before you."

Florence was crushed.

"You're about as sexy as a bag of toenail clippings," he said coldly. "And besides, I'm married. Granted I don't love her and I'm leaving her behind, but legally, I'm married. Hell, I'd sleep with my own wife before I'd have sex with you." And with that, Peyton Pomp pushed Florence out of the doorway and exited the building.

She looked out of the office window with tears streaming down her face, as he raced off in his car. After three years of selflessly devoting herself to her job and to Peyton Pomp, and knowing very well that he was a corrupt and despicable man, never had she ever seen him be so cruel and heartless to another person. Right then and there she vowed to herself that she would have every married man in Ragland thinking she was the hottest and sexiest woman he'd ever met.

Florence left town and promptly had her yellow teeth laminated white, her nonexistent breasts enlarged to a thirty-six triple "D", her mousy hair bleached blonde, and acid poured over her acne scarred face to smooth it out. However, she kept her trademark black horn-rimmed glasses, which she felt gave her an air of intelligence, and she returned seven years later. The former Miss Bovine of Tomorrow was transformed into Dr. Belle Pepper of today.

And now, at age fifty-five, she fancied herself the most sought-after sexual therapist in Ragland, albeit the only sexual therapist in Ragland. Her price was high and her skin was thick and no one would ever reach her heart again.

*   *   *   *

Bursting with excitement, Junior looked at his watch and counted, "Eight, seven, six, five, four, three, two!"

He opened the office door, and there was standing Beufort Bodman, buttoning up his shirt.

A flood of emotions struck Junior. First, he was surprised. Then confused, then angry, and then jealous.

"Beufort," he acknowledged.

"Junior."

"Goodbye Beufort," hollered the doctor from her bathroom. "See you next week."

Beufort dropped a hundred-dollar bill on the table next to the door. Junior snorted like a bull as Beufort slipped by him and out the door.

"Hello?" Junior called out as he shut and locked the door.

"Junior? Junior Martindale? Is that you?" Belle said, as she came out of the bathroom. She wore a tight red dress and was pinning her hair back up into a French twist.

"I didn't know you were seeing Beufort Bodman."

Belle slipped on her glasses. "I see a lot of patients. And I warned you not to come...early." She smiled seductively at him acknowledging her double entendre. "Sit down. Relax. Don't get yourself all worked up...yet."

Junior took his coat off and looked at her as she sat down in her Naugahyde chair. She freshened her red lipstick.

"So Junior, have you implemented any of the techniques you've learned here with me at home with your wife?"

"No. We haven't connected yet." Still angry, he asked, "What kind of counselor are you, Dr. Pepper?"

"We've been through this before Junior. I'm a professional."

"A professional what?"

"Esoteric Counselor for the enlightened few."

"I'm not quite sure I know what that means."

"Am I helping you or not, Junior? Are you and your wife... talking more, now?"

"Yes. No. I mean, she is."

"Tell me, if she were here right now, what would you say to her?" Before he could respond, she repositioned herself in her oversized chair. "Have you explained to her how erotic listening can be?"

"Uh..."

"Does she know how much she's missing out on when, in the throes of foreplay, you could be talking, describing how hot, how sexy, how irresistible her body is?"

"Uh…"

She shifted her body and took off her glasses.

"Let's role play again, Junior."

"OK, Dr. Pepper."

"Please? I told you to call me Belle."

"Yes…Belle Pepper."

"Sweet, not hot?"

"Oh, uh, sweet and hot!"

"And remember Junior, we are doing this all within the context of your emotional, intellectual and physical healing with your wife, Cloris."

"Cl-Cl-Clairese."

She took out her hairpin, and her blonde curls cascaded down, over her shoulders.

"Go on and talk to me. Talk me up a storm."

"Awww, Belle. You're beautiful."

"Clairissa."

"Clairese."

"Go on, Mr. Man."

"Ah, your hair looks so soft and I'm sure it smells so good."

"You'd like to smell it, wouldn't you?"

"Yes, Ma'am."

"Tell me more, big guy."

"Your lips are full and glossed. I wish I could kiss them."

She licked them.

"I want to tease your mouth with my lips. I want to run my fingers down your neck and stop at that hollow."

Taking her out of the moment, she asked, "What hollow?"

"The one in the ridge of your collar bone?"

"Where is that?"

He pointed to the hollow in his neck.

"Oh, OK. You can continue."

"I don't kiss it. I gently blow on it."

Belle was beginning to writhe with pleasure and started unbuttoning her blouse.

"Oh Belle. Oh Belle."

"Chlorine."

"Clairese."

She repositioned herself in the chair and the back of her thigh stuck to the Naugahyde. She pulled it away and it made a suction sound.

"Oh yes, Junior. Oh yes."

He couldn't help himself and started ripping his clothes off. "I'm going to take you."

"Yeah, baby."

"I'm going to take you the way you want me to take you."

"Come on, lover boy. You want this?" she cooed as she ran her fingers over her breasts. "You want this?"

"Yes, it's mine."

"Then claim it, baby. Claim it!"

Junior dropped his pants and stepped towards her, tripping, falling on his face, right at her feet.

She slipped a shoe off and they made contact. Her bunion against his cheek. He sniffed her foot, rolled his eyes and then started kissing her toes.

"This little piggy went to the market," he said in a little boy's voice. "This little piggy stayed home."

Belle was squirming with delight.

"This little piggy had roast beef. This little piggy had none." He paused.

"And? And?"

"And this little piggy ran all the way home!"

Junior climbed up onto Belle and the chair fell over backwards. They started rolling around on the floor. He was on top. She was on top. Twisting, turning, writhing, moaning.

Junior cried, "I want you, Belle. I want you more than any other woman. I'm going to claim you now. No one else can touch you. I'm claiming you!"

"Prove it, big boy."

"I'm leaving my wife…"

Belle stopped instantly. "What?"

"And I'm going to marry you."

"What?" asked Belle not sure of what she had just heard.

"I love you Belle. Marry me?"

"No."

Junior continued to ravish her.

"Stop! Stop it right now, Junior. Time out!"

He rolled off her. "Why? What's wrong?"

"Transference."

"What?" panted Junior.

"Pull yourself together."

"What went wrong?"

Belle picked herself up off the floor. She put her glasses back on, pulled down her dress and then righted the chair as Junior got to his feet.

"Junior, you totally misunderstand my work. It's time we parted."

"But? But?" he said zipping up his fly.

"I'm sorry, but this will be our last session. Go home to your wife."

"Fuck my wife! I want you and I know you want me. I love you."

"Who do you think I am?"

"Belle Pepper?"

"Dr. Pepper. I am a professional. You must go now and not return."

"Geez."

"And do not speak to anyone of this. I have my reputation to think of."

"Gol-ly!" Totally confused, he started to leave.

"And Junior?"

He turned around. "Yes?"

"Leave the hundred dollars on the table by the door."

She stood by the bathroom door as Junior counted out four twenty-dollar bills and then twenty singles and laid them on top of Beufort's hundred.

He opened the door. Feeling totally dejected, he glanced back at her. She turned her head away and he left.

Still trying to digest what had happened, he walked to his car, which had a parking ticket stuck to the windshield.

"Shit," he cried.

TEN

FORTY, BARREN AND NOBODY'S FAVORITE

Lex, with a dishpan full of warm water and a face cloth, gently knocked on Bert's door.

"Dad?" He stuck his head in. "You awake?"

Bert, lying on his back, slowly looked over at Lex and winked.

"Hey," Lex said softly. He walked in, pulled a chair up next to the bed and sat the pan down on it. "Nice and quiet right now." Bert blinked again.

Knowing how much his father loved silence, Lex gracefully gave him a sponge bath, without speaking a word.

As Bert watched him, he realized how much Lex looked like him as a young man. How strange he thought time was. Bert was quite aware of his life's coming to an end, and yet he felt he hadn't really started. Spending so much of his life disappointed about the past and worrying about the future, he now regretted that it had kept him from living in the moment. Where had the time gone?

All thought that Bert was brave and stoic, but he was scared shitless. And although he now looked and acted much older than his sixty-eight years, Bert still felt like a vulnerable child.

Both Trudy Lee and Bert were only children. Depression children. No brothers. No sisters. Therefore their children had no aunts, uncles or cousins.

Seeing his father smile, Lex felt good knowing that it was because of the warm water. In truth, Bert sensed that the Martindale name would probably come to an end soon. And it gave him a chuckle inside, thinking that it was for the best. They had done enough damage on this earth. Bert focused on the giant map of the world on the opposite wall and struggled to take a deep breath.

"I know," soothed Lex. "It feels good."

Again, Bert looked up at him. Being the caretaker type, like Lex, it was humiliating that his own children had to bathe, feed and dress him at this point in his life.

He looked at Lex's profile, which reminded him of his own mother, Willa Lyons. He tried to count how many years it had been since he had thought of her. Many, since her memories brought back so much pain.

* * * *

"Bertrand?" hollered his mother. "Bertrand, dinner's ready."

Bert, being an extroverted child, was always putting some sort of neighborhood game together. Growing up in Ragland during the depression, a child had to be quite resourceful. There were the usual games all the kids played. Tag, hide-and-go-seek and baseball. But he liked one in particular called Beckin's Wanted. Basically kick the can, but played with teams and strategies.

As he was a natural athlete and leader, even at the young age of nine, everyone in the neighborhood turned to Bert for organization.

"Bertrand," yelled Willa. "Come on, child. It's getting cold!"

Obeying his mother's calls, he left the gang and ran across his front lawn and into their house.

Bert's father, Franklin, was a quiet man. He owned a local bar-
bershop and a pool hall. And unbeknownst to Bert and his
mother, he was quite the womanizer. So, between Franklin's work
and his sexual appetite, Bert never really saw his father much.

"You're gonna read and do your homework after dinner, right,
Bertrand?"

"Yes, Ma'am," he said with a mouth full of fried chicken. Bert
loved his books as much as he did sports, so he was happy to
spend the night studying.

"Aunt Tessie's due any day now and Uncle Stewie is working
late so I'm going next door to tend to her needs, OK?"

"Yes, Ma'am."

"Don't know what time your father will be in."

"OK."

"So, if I'm late, Bertrand, you close down the house and get
into bed."

"Yes, Ma'am," he said as Willa gave him a kiss.

"Goodbye, son."

"Bye Mamma."

After finishing his dinner, Bert put his plate in the sink and
ran into his bedroom. The walls of his room were covered with
maps. Faraway places he dreamed of traveling to. Destinations
like China and Africa. Australia and India. Japan and Europe.

But as he was doing his math homework, he heard a lot of
commotion next door at Aunt Tessie's. He looked out of his window and saw his mother helping her very pregnant sister into the
back seat of her car. Bert rushed out of the house and over to the
driveway.

"Everything OK, Mamma?"

"Yes, dear. Just taking Aunt Tessie to the hospital."

Bert tried to look into the car as Willa jumped into the driver's
seat.

"Step back, Bertrand," his mother hollered. "She's having the
baby. We're in a real hurry, here."

Neighborhood children gathered in front of Aunt Tessie's house as they watched Bert's mother try to engage the clutch of her sister's car. Frightened of automobiles, Willa never did drive much.

She managed to back out of Tessie's driveway, squashing only half of her flower garden. Once on Rattlesnake Road, Willa struggled to shift the car into forward and jerked it down the street.

Willa was driving slowly enough so that Bert could run along side.

"You're doing great, Mamma."

She nervously looked out her window at Bert. "Get back, dear. This is a dangerous vehicle!"

Bert laughed as he followed them down to the railroad tracks.

There was a slight incline in the road at the intersection and as Willa approached it, the car stalled.

"Damn," she cried. She jerked the brakes on and started the engine again.

Bert watched from the side of the road as she tried to make the incline, once more. But his attention was diverted to the train whistle down the track.

Willa had control of the car and sped up the incline. But once she was at the crest, she eased up on the gas pedal and the back wheels locked into the railroad tracks.

"Mamma?" yelled Bert. "Rock the car! Put on the gas!"

Willa panicked as she heard the whistle herself. Bert started running to the tracks but everything seemed as though it were moving in slow motion; everything but the train.

With the car stuck on the tracks, she made the decision to jump out and pull Tessie to safety. But as Bert held his breath, neither of them moved fast enough.

The train blew its whistle and even screeched on its brakes, but it was too late. Bert watched in horror as his mother and Aunt Tessie were struck down by the train.

The funeral was devastating for Bert. The nightmare of the accident kept running over and over in his mind, nearly driving him mad, like a loose shutter incessantly banging against the house during a windstorm. Feeling it was his fault that he couldn't save his mother and aunt, Bert didn't speak for weeks. The once outgoing boy was now an introvert.

He took care of the house and did some of the cooking, but his father came home less and less. So, at the age of fifteen, Bert went off to work in a coal mine. He worked and studied hard, excelled in school and went to college on scholarships.

But he was changed, forever. The mother he loved was killed right before his eyes. Bert never healed from that experience. And he never went to any of the far-away places he once had dreamed of, either. Not China or Africa. Australia or India. Japan or Europe. Bert stayed in North Carolina for the rest of his life.

*　*　*　*

Lex washed Bert's brow, and having thought that he'd got soap in his eyes, wiped away the tears that were streaming down his father's cheeks.

"Sorry," Lex whispered as he dabbed at them. "I didn't mean to hurt you."

Back in the moment, Bert looked up at Lex and cried harder. Realizing this, Lex put down the washcloth and looked at his father. Not knowing if he should hold him or leave, they just stared at one another.

Seconds felt like eternities till Mona Lee called out from the keeping room. "Lex?"

Bert turned his head away and Lex left the room with the dishpan.

"How's Dad?" she asked while sucking on a lemon.

"I just gave him a bath." Walking back into the kitchen allowed Lex a few moments to pull himself together.

171

She paused for a moment as she watched him pour the water out into the kitchen sink and clean the pan.

"You all hate me."

"What?"

"Do you like me?"

Lex turned around and looked at her. "What kind of question is that?"

"Direct. Do you like me?"

He thought about it. "I love you."

"But do you like me?"

He shrugged his shoulders. "I'd like to like you."

"But do you like me?"

She pushed him too far. "No God damn it, I don't like you. There, I said it."

She thought about it for a moment. "Why don't you like me?"

"God, Mona Lee!"

"Be blunt. I can take it."

He dried off his hands. "Well, you…"

"Yes?"

"You have…"

"Yes, I have what?"

"Well, Mona Lee, you have an edge."

She shouted, "What the hell does that mean?"

He thought to himself, *How could such a loud voice come out of such a small woman?* "You always seem to be angry about something."

"Well, I am. I'm mad. I'm real mad!"

Lex threw his arms up into the air. "But why, Mona Lee? Why?"

She literally walked around in circles. "I'm mad at Mother for being so weak. I'm mad at Roscoe for having a drinking problem. I'm mad at Junior for being such a wuss. I'm mad at Daddy for dying like this. I'm mad that we weren't born into money and royalty."

He was honestly surprised. "Gee, I had no idea."

She stopped circling and pointed her finger right at him. "And I'm real mad at you for being so nice. So polite. So understanding. You always see both sides. You're always straddling the fence."

"I wasn't aware…"

She actually poked him with her finger. "And you're perfect. Your life is perfect. Everything comes to you so easy."

He turned away from her and said as calmly as possible, "That's the farthest thing from the truth."

She spun him around. "See, you say that so intellectual like. Why don't you scream at me, for God's sake?"

Lex took a breath and said even calmer, "I'm not going to fight with you, Mona Lee."

"You don't fool me, Alexi Lee Martindale. I know what you're doing. You play the rational father so you feel like you're the one in control. God, I hate it. It's so condescending. Look at you. You're so frightened of confrontation."

"I'm warning you, Mona Lee."

She stood on her tippy-toes and tried to put her face into his, but managed to reach mid-chest. "What are you going to do? Run home crying to your boyfriend?"

"Stop acting like a child, Midge."

She reached up and slapped him across the face. In a flash, he hit her right back. Both shocked, they stood there a second and she tried to hit him again. Lex grabbed her wrists.

"How dare you call me that?"

"Everyone else does."

Lex wrestled her so that he had her arm around her back. They were pressed up against each other, her back to his front.

"But they don't mean it. You meant it."

"Mona Lee, sometimes you get me so mad, I start to shake inside and I think I'm going to kill!"

She was intrigued and stopped wrestling for a moment. "Really?"

Lex relaxed his grip and she spun around hitting him. He tripped her leg and she fell to the floor. Lex jumped on top of Mona Lee. She was lying on her back and he was straddling her chest, pinning down her arms with his hands.

"Get off of me, Lex. You're hurting me."

"Oh, and you haven't hurt me?"

"What are you talking about?"

He brought his face down close to hers. "Just look at our home movies, Mona Lee. When we were kids you were always pushing me out of view or knocking me down or sitting on my face."

"You're being stupid."

"When I entered the seventh grade I remember seeing you in the cafeteria. All your friends trailing behind you. Think hard, Mona Lee. Do you ever remember friends trailing behind me? And when I saw you, I brought my tray over and sat next to you. I was so proud to be your brother. And then you got up and said to your friends, 'let's find a clear table.' And you left me. I skipped lunch for the rest of the year. Do you know what I used to love more than anything else in the world? Playing the piano. And yet, to this day, every time I sit down to play I hear your voice. 'Well, I used to like that song.'"

He rolled off of Mona Lee and onto the floor.

"Lex, you can't hold me responsible for what happened when we were kids."

"That's right. And you can't hold the family responsible for what you don't have in your life, today."

"But you always got what you needed. You're Mother's favorite."

"And you...were...Dad's."

"Were is the operative word, Lex. I'm nobody's favorite. Nobody's! I'm forty, barren and nobody's favorite!"

Exhausted, Lex started to laugh.

"Mona Lee, you are very, very funny."

She couldn't help but giggle.

Just then Trudy Lee entered the screen porch, proudly wearing a new hat. Hearing Lex and Mona Lee laughing together, she quietly put down her shopping bags. She smiled and watched them, unnoticed through the doorway.

"Stop Lex. It's no laughing matter."

They both laughed harder.

"OK, you want to be Mother's favorite? It means being her best friend, her confidante, her playmate, her shrink, her parent. Trudy Lee has never been a mother for me."

Crushed, Trudy Lee couldn't believe what she was hearing.

Lex continued. "I have never had the luxury of running up to her and saying, 'Mommy, help me. Mommy, I'm hurt. Mommy, I'm sick.' Or would you rather be Dad's favorite, again? 'Good daughter! Throw that shot put a little farther this time. Open your stride during the last 220. Yes, daughter. Good, daughter.'"

Bert banged his cup in his bedroom.

Mona Lee and Lex were silent for a moment and then broke out into hysterical laughter.

"Oh my God, Lex," she screamed as she held onto her belly.

"What is it?"

"I'm having an accident! Right now, I'm having an accident!"

She got up off the floor and bolted up the back staircase, gripping her gut, as Trudy Lee barged in with the groceries and made a bee-line for the kitchen.

Lex was still on the floor catching his breath as he called out to her. "Mother?"

Ignoring him, she dropped the groceries on the counter and whipped off the hat. Her hair was brown.

"Mother, your hair."

He panicked, not knowing how long she had been standing there. "Mother?"

She angrily threw grocery items into cupboards.

"Mother? Are you all right?" He got up and walked over to her. "Where's Grandma Battles? Is she over at Clairese's?"

She took several potatoes out of the fridge.

"Mother, I'm sorry you heard that."

Trudy Lee scavenged through a drawer, found a peeler and started stripping the potatoes to death.

"Ah come on. You can't be mad at me. The point is we're best friends. Well, we are, aren't we? Mother, don't do this. Don't play the silent game. I hate it. You know I can't take it. Mother, please talk to me!"

She slowly turned to him, cold as ice. "You want me to talk to you? Well, here goes, Mother's favorite. You betrayed me. You laughed at me. So, you think I'm everything but a mother to you? Who nursed you when you had the measles? Who stayed with you day and night when you had your allergic reaction to penicillin? Who saved your life when you stepped on a hornet's nest and got stung one hundred and fifty-two times? I did!"

"I know Mother. I'm sorry. I didn't mean what I said. It's just that Mona Lee got me going."

"And all this time I thought I could trust you."

"You can trust me. Honest. I just said that stuff to shut her up. Please forgive me."

She turned back to the potatoes and started peeling. "Well, I think that stinks. Going around telling people what they want to hear instead of what you think. You must have picked that one up from your father because I always tell the truth."

"Or your version of it," he whispered under his breath.

She turned back to him quickly. "What was that?"

"Nothing."

"It's so easy for you all to criticize me behind my back."

Exhausted, sleep deprived and hung over from his migraine, Lex started rubbing his head. "Stop. Please, let's just stop."

She threw the potato peeler into the stainless steel sink. "No, I don't want to stop! No one has a clue as to what I'm going through. I haven't had a decent night's sleep in three months. My life here is a nightmare and I get no support from anyone. Not even you. I'm at my wits end, Lex. I know I'm just moments away from having a nervous breakdown, and not one person cares. Not one!"

"That's not true. I care."

"Well, you could have fooled me."

"You know how much I care."

She turned away from him.

"Mother, this isn't the time to argue. Please forgive me."

He walked towards her, perplexed as to what to do. He gently touched her back. Slowly, she turned around and they embraced.

"Thank you," he said, as she started to cry.

"Oh Lex, I'm sorry."

"It's OK."

"I never could stay mad at you for very long."

"There, there," he said rubbing her back.

"I'm trying so hard. Really I am."

"We all are. We're all trying so hard."

She cried harder.

"Ssshhhh. Ssshhhh. Everything will be all right. I promise."

She smiled as they embraced a moment longer, and then Trudy Lee pulled away quickly.

"Lex, what's the matter with you? You're shaking."

Suddenly, his legs buckled and she caught him.

"Mother?"

"Lex!"

She walked him into the keeping room and sat him down on the loveseat. "Darling, you have a rash on your neck."

"Yes."

She felt his forehead.

"Are you sick? You're so pale. Is it another migraine? Is it an allergic reaction? Lex, please talk to me. Is there something wrong?"

"Yes, something is wrong."

"Well, what is it?"

"I tried to tell you earlier, but…"

"But what?"

He looked up at her frightened face. "Mother, I have…"

"Oh dear God, please tell me it's not serious."

"I have…I haven't eaten a thing today."

There was a moment of silence and then Trudy Lee burst into nervous laughter.

"Oh, you silly thing." She threw her arms around him desperately. "If that's all it is, let me fix you something. Oh, how about your favorite sandwich? A reuben!"

"Do you know what I need first? My tote bag from upstairs. Could you get it for me?"

"Of course. You just lie down and I'll be right back. And we can have a couple of ice cold beers and maybe there's a good movie on television. Oh, we'll have so much fun."

She ran up the stairs as fast as she could, hiding the tears that were beginning to fall. The moment Trudy Lee was out of Lex's sight she slumped against the hallway wall. Unable to control her fear, she let out a gasp and then covered her mouth with her hand.

"So much fun," Lex said to himself.

Dog-tired, Lex lay down, when suddenly Bert appeared at the keeping room doorway. He managed to take a few more steps forward and then began to wobble.

"Aaaaaaahhh!" he screamed out.

Lex bolted upright. "Dad!"

"Aaaaaaahhh!"

Lex jumped off the loveseat and caught Bert just as he was collapsing. He gently lowered him to the floor.

"Dad?"

Bert twisted from side to side.

"Oh my God, Mother," Lex screamed. "Mona Lee!"

Bert started moaning. Thinking he was in physical pain, Lex stroked his hair to calm him down. But Bert had heard every word Trudy Lee wouldn't let Lex say.

"Just relax, Dad. Just relax. That's it. I know. I know. It's hard. I'm not feeling too good myself."

Bert's body tensed up. He so wanted to take care of Lex, but all he could do was look up at him.

"I'm OK. I'm OK. Don't worry. Just relax."

Bert stared at him as Lex gently rocked him.

"Remember when I went on your business trip with you to Hartford? Gosh, I must have been Mattie Lee's age. We stayed at the Howard Johnson's Motor Lodge across from Top's Toy Fair. And when you went off to your meeting I ran over and bought a magic set with money I had saved. Learned all the tricks and then sat in the hotel room for hours watching the clock, just waiting for you to come back so I could show you what I had learned." He paused. "I wish I could perform some magic right now."

Bert smiled.

"I love you, Dad."

Bert managed to lift his arm up to Lex's face. He touched it and then fell asleep.

"Keep breathing, Alexi Lee," he whispered to himself. "It's essential to life."

ELEVEN

THE HOLY TRINITY

Late that afternoon, Grandma Battles could be heard laughing from Mattie Lee's bedroom up in the Slaves' Quarters.

"My mamma hates sex," whispered Mattie Lee to Anastasia.

"Did she tell you that?"

"No, I heard her say it to Daddy. I hear everything they say in their bedroom."

Unaware that she had subjected Trudy Lee to the same inappropriate behavior, Anastasia shook her head with disapproval. "That's so wrong."

"Mamma says that sex is unsanitary."

"Poor Junior," laughed Anastasia. "Sex can be wonderful, darling. Sometimes romantic. Sometimes kinky."

Mattie Lee's eyes opened wide. "Does it hurt?"

"It can in the beginning, for some people. It's kinda like riding a bicycle."

Mattie Lee shifted her butt. "Then I think my mamma must need training wheels."

Anastasia laughed again. "Once you get the hang of it, it's a lot of fun. And I'm really good at it, if I say so myself," she said grinning from ear to ear.

Mattie Lee moved a little closer to her. "Are you still dating Duke up in Detroit?"

"Nah, Duke died."

"Oh Grandma, I'm so sorry."

"Don't be. It was his time and he lived a long and good life." Anastasia leaned in towards Mattie Lee. "He died…while we were doing it," she confided. The wonderful thought of it made her snort with laughter and almost fall over.

"Wow, you must be good."

"No complaints yet," she smiled.

It just dawned on Mattie Lee. "Oh, so that's why you said bright colors attract men. You're available, again."

"You better believe it."

"So, is this a generic thing?"

Anastasia was confused. "What dear?"

"You and Trudy Lee being so sexual. Will I be like that, too?"

"You mean genetic. Maybe. Maybe not. Granted, Trudy Lee was out of control early on in her adult life, but once she went through menopause, she's been all talk and no action. But not me. Sex all the time," she said proudly.

"So, how old were you when you first did it, Grandma?"

The question took Anastasia so far back in time. "I was a good girl and a late bloomer. I had sex for the first time on my honeymoon. And I was madly in love with him."

"Papa Battles?"

Anastasia pondered this for a moment and then looked at Mattie Lee. "Would you like the story I tell everyone or would you like the truth?"

"The truth?" she asked hesitantly.

"OK. I always thought I'd take this with me to my grave, but as that time gets closer, I feel the urge more and more to unburden myself. Get it off my chest. And I think I can trust you with it."

"Of course you can."

"All right, but you must swear on the Holy Bible. Well, you've already done that." They both giggled. "You must promise me that you will never ever tell anyone."

Mattie Lee outlined her chest with an X. "Cross my heart and hope to die, stick a needle in my eye."

"That always sounds so gruesome. Let's just shake on it."

"It's a deal," Mattie Lee said as they shook hands. "Now, tell me. Tell me!"

"Well, I met Papa Battles in the spring of 1925."

* * * *

"Stasia?" hollered her mother from her bedside while recuperating from another blinding migraine. "Stasia King, where's my lunch?"

Nineteen-year-old Anastasia felt like an old woman.

Her younger sister Gertie folded another sheet with yet another sister, Helen. "Stasia, you were supposed to pick up Mrs. Swampscott's laundry an hour ago."

By the early twenties, the family had given up on farming. Actually, farming had given up on them and had forced them to sell twenty acres of the lower fields just to stay alive. Nathaniel had turned to amateur fighting to make extra money, but shockingly had died one year later, due to a brain hemorrhage suffered from a boxing match. And although it was Anastasia's mother Dilly who had dreamed up the idea of a laundry service, Anastasia was the one who had to make it happen.

It was mid-July and Ragland was in the middle of a grueling heat wave. To add to that, Terror's kitchen and keeping room, where they were doing all of the hand washing and ironing, had no ventilation. The windows and doors were open wide but the air was completely stagnant. Nothing was moving.

Neither was Stasia. Exhausted and hungry, she looked at the iron heating up on the stove, and her eyes began to cross, she was so overworked.

Stasia picked the hot iron off the stove, pressed it onto Mr. Mundy's white dress shirt, and promptly, fell asleep.

"Stasia," screamed Gertie. "Stasia, you're burning it!"

Having dozed off for just a second, she jerked awake and started pressing. Her right shoulder had already developed premature rheumatoid arthritis from the constant motion of pushing backwards and forwards.

"Stop Stasia," continued Gertie. "It's tearing all up!"

Stasia snapped out of it and realized what she had done.

"That's the third shirt this week you've ruined," scolded Gertie. "Ma's going to have a fit."

They could hear her hollering from her bed. "Where's my lunch?"

Stasia looked at Gertie, the ruined shirt, two of her siblings running through the kitchen, the soup boiling over on the stove and then ran out into the backyard. Gertie followed.

"I can't take it," Stasia cried as she sat down on a crate in between lines of clothes drying. "I can't take it anymore."

Her eleven-year-old brother Johnny came over and sat next to her and Gertie.

"I just can't take it anymore."

"I'm sorry, Stasia," Johnny said handing her the edge of a sheet trying to dry in the humid air.

Stasia wiped away her tears, looked at him and messed up his hair. "It's not your fault, kiddo."

She started to cry again. "Why the hell did this happen to me?"

"Stasia," Gertie said all excited, "I have an extra ticket to see the Winston-Salem Lions play against the Detroit Tigers on Saturday. Please come with Ray and me."

"But who's gonna...," Stasia looked at the laundry, poked Johnny, pointed at three other children running in and out of the sheets, gestured to her mother in the house and then just threw up her arms.

"Claire's fifteen now. I've already talked to her, and she offered to hold down the fort long enough for us to get away for the day."

"Claire? Our sister, the prima donna, offered?"

"Well, I'm paying her. But it's worth it, Stasia. Please come with us. Ray's got his Pa's car."

She thought about it and then wiped her sweaty brow, deciding, "Why not?"

Soccer teams sponsored by big corporations were very popular back then, as big as football teams are today. After World War I, a trucking corporation named Starwood recruited identical twins, Kyle and Karl Battles, from Scotland, to play for the Winston-Salem Lions.

Stasia had never been to a soccer game nor had any interest in it. But the moment she saw the Battles twins come out onto the field, she was hooked.

"Oh, my, Gertie," she panted all out of breath. "Look at them. God's gift to women!"

"And he made two of them," whispered Gertie so Ray couldn't hear her. "Two of them."

"They are so handsome," sighed Stasia. "And so sexy in those uniforms with their lean upper bodies and thick muscular legs. Mmmm."

Gertie smiled as she saw her older sister enjoying herself for the first time in months. Ray knew one of the soccer players, so they all went around to the men's locker room door after the match to say hello. And while they were waiting, who should come out but Kyle Battles, and wham, Anastasia knew she was in love. Instantly!

"Hands off him," Gertie whispered. "That one's married with kids."

Even so, Kyle gazed right at Stasia and smiled. She was quite the looker back then. And suddenly she saw Karl. He, too was gorgeous, but something was different about him. As light and easygoing as Kyle was, Karl was dark and moody and a chain smoker.

That summer, Stasia and Gertie spent all of their savings running down to Winston-Salem with Ray to watch the Lions play soccer anytime they could to get away from the chores at home. And each time, they would stop by the locker room door and say hello to the twins.

On one trip, Karl asked Stasia to dinner. She couldn't remember the last time she had gone out on a date.

"Yes," she said too eagerly. "I'd love to."

So, Karl and Stasia and Gertie and Ray started double dating. One thing led to another and before Stasia knew it, Karl had asked her to marry him.

She hesitated only for a second. She knew this could be her ticket out of Ragland. She was worn out from running the business and mothering the children. Her first choice would have been Kyle. But since he was already taken, she thought to herself, *If I can't have Kyle, well, I'll take second best.*

Against her mother's wishes, Anastasia King and Karl Battles were married by a justice of the peace on the soccer field in Winston-Salem, North Carolina on September 1, 1925.

Their honeymoon had to be spent on tour with the ball team. In fact, they left that night for Peoria, Illinois. They stayed in room number 606 at the Carter Hotel. Kyle had 608, the room next door. Kyle traveled without his family, due to the fact that they had two children and another one on the way.

Anastasia couldn't believe how happy she was. She was free and married and staying in a hotel for the first time in her life. And knowing how romantic and sweet Karl could be, she fantasized about how wonderful their first time together would be. But he got drunk at the reception, and once up in their room, he was cold and furious with her.

"Karl?" Stasia asked frightened she might make him angrier. "Is it something I did? Is it something I didn't do?"

"Let's just do it and get it over with," he growled, as he jumped on top of Anastasia.

"Stop it. Karl, stop it!"

Anastasia struggled but he was too strong. He jabbed himself inside her, had a very quick ejaculation and then rolled off.

She cried and ran into the bathroom to take a shower, as he lit another cigarette. Anastasia stood under the water hoping to rinse away the pain and disappointment. The moment he had that ring on Stasia's finger he changed. Just like that. He didn't want to kiss her. He didn't want to hold her. It's as though, all of a sudden, he hated her. In hindsight, Anastasia believed Karl sensed her attraction to Kyle and married her out of spite.

When she finally came out of the bathroom, Karl had passed out. She quickly got dressed and went down to the hotel's bar to buy a stiff drink. Eyes puffy from crying, she sat down at the end of the Carter Hotel bar and ordered herself a bourbon. As she was taking her money out to pay the bartender, someone put his hand on top of hers. Thinking it was Karl, her body tensed up and she looked away.

"Stasia?" he said. And she realized it was Kyle.

She didn't have to say a word. He knew his brother better than anyone. He just wrapped his arms around her as she sobbed.

"Oh Kyle," she cried. "I've made an awful mistake."

"It's OK. Just let it out."

She cried harder as she fell into her husband's brother's arms. No words spoken, the two of them went back upstairs to his room and made love. Deep, passionate love.

Afterwards, Kyle confessed to Stasia that he had fallen out of love with his wife. They made love again and then she fell asleep in his arms. But around three in the morning both were awakened by the sounds of fire trucks. Smoke was coming in under the hotel room door.

"The door's hot!" Kyle yelled as he felt it. "Fire! We can't open it!"

As they climbed out of the window and onto the escape, a fire ladder was already reaching up to their floor. Anastasia turned to look back at Karl's room and saw flames leaping out.

"Karl," she whispered.

But the firemen pulled Kyle and Stasia onto the fire ladder and they were brought down to safety.

And when the fire was put out, Karl's body was discovered. He had set his room on fire with a cigarette.

*　*　*　*

"That's so tragic, Grandma," Mattie Lee exclaimed. But then she thought. "Hey, but Grandpa Battles name was...Karl."

"Yes dear. It was. Everything in our rooms was destroyed. Including Kyle and Karl's personal documents. In a flash, we read each other's minds, and from that moment on, Kyle took over Karl's identity."

"Oh my gosh!"

"He felt for his wife and loved his kids and took great care of them, emotionally and financially. That's the main reason we never had any money left over. He was supporting two families."

"But you really loved him, right?"

"Yes, dear. And he loved me and I got my man. And nine months later, Trudy Lee was born."

Mattie Lee paused again, to think. "So Grandma? Who's her father?"

"I don't know, darling. It could be Kyle or it could be Karl."

Mattie Lee shook her head with disbelief. "Fascinating. I wish I had known Papa Battles."

"He was a real pistol, Mattie Lee. And God, do I miss him. I loved that man with all my heart and never cheated on him. But that doesn't mean I wasn't a vicious flirt. But once he was gone, boy did I have fun."

"You are too much, Grandma."

Stasia hugged her. "I'll take that as a compliment. So, if you can, wait till you're in love to have sex."

"OK."

"And if there's one thing I've learned in my old age, it's that when you think you have everything figured out, fate throws you a curve ball and you just gotta go with the punches."

Outside, a car pulled up to Terror and honked its horn. Lex awoke from a nap and looked out of the upstairs bedroom window and saw Joey Tisbit getting out of his police cruiser. He had in his hand Roscoe's boot.

"Damn," Lex whispered to himself as he opened the window. "Hey, Joey."

"Lex, good to see you, guy," he said shouting up to him.

"Don't knock on the door. Dad's asleep. I'll be right down."

"Sure thing," he whispered.

Lex ran out of the bedroom and flew down the back stairs and out the screen porch.

"Down from New York?" Joey asked.

They shook hands. "Yeah," Lex said all out of breath. "How's your family and all?"

"Not too bad. I heard your Pa's not doing too well?"

Lex looked back at the house. "He's hanging in there. Hanging in there."

"I hate to bring this up now and all, but, seems as though we got a call from Delbert Lovejoy."

Lex tried to act surprised. "Oh really?"

"A complaint about someone snooping around on his property last night."

"No kidding?"

He held the boot out to Lex. "You don't happen to know who this might belong to, do you Lex?"

"Gee, Joey. It looks like a million other work boots to me."

"Well, best you keep your doors locked tonight. Strange times we're living in now."

Lex put his hand on the officer's shoulder. "Good advice, Joey,"

Lex said, guiding him back towards his car.

Suddenly, Trudy Lee came out of the screen porch. "Hi Officer Tisbit," she said, adding a layer of lipstick.

Lex looked up to the heavens.

"Hello, Mrs. Martindale. Ma'am."

"Any trouble, Sir?"

Lex cut in. "No mother, there is no trouble."

"Hey, isn't that Roscoe's boot?" she said pointing to Joey's hand.

Lex dropped his head.

"He's been looking for that all day."

"Mother, Joey, ah, Officer Tisbit said that Delbert Lovejoy found the boot on his property last night."

"Last night?" she asked.

"That's right, Ma'am. Someone was snooping around on his property."

"Is that so?" Trudy Lee asked as she looked hard at Lex. "Hmmm," she pondered. "I think then it must have been…"

Lex held his breath.

"Roscoe."

Lex looked at her.

"He was three sheets to the wind last night," she said. "He must have thought their house was ours. I believe he's done that before."

"Yeah," agreed Lex. "He's really been stressed about my dad and all."

"Well, here's his boot. I'm going to try to talk Delbert outta pressing charges. Sounds innocent to me."

"Oh, Roscoe wouldn't hurt a flea," added Lex.

"Not a flea," Trudy Lee agreed with a mischievous grin.

Officer Tisbit got back into his car. "I'll be off. And I sure hope Mr. Martindale feels better soon."

"Thanks, Joey," Lex said closing his door for him.

"Bye, Officer Tisbit," flirted Trudy Lee. "Thanks for returning

Roscoe's boot."

"Just doing my job, Ma'am."

"And a good one at that," added Lex. "Bye now."

Officer Tisbit started up his cruiser and drove off, waving goodbye.

"Imagine that?" Lex said as he ran back towards the house.

Trudy Lee looked at the boot and then at Lex, suspiciously. "Hmmm, imagine that?" she repeated following him into the house as Mattie Lee helped Grandma Battles out of the Slaves' Quarters.

"Thanks for the advice, Grandma. And telling me about sex and all."

"Anytime, dear. So, how many Hail Marys did Father Ken have you recite?"

The two of them slowly made their way towards Terror. "Just a hundred. And I have to stay after Sunday school and do clean-up for a month."

"That doesn't sound too bad."

"Psssst. Mattie Lee!" Lowell hollered from the stone wall.

"Who's that?" asked Anastasia looking around.

"Lover boy," laughed Mattie Lee.

"Be gentle with him, Mattie Lee. And tell him the truth about the birds and the bees."

"OK." She made sure Grandma Battles was safely in the screen porch and then she ran back to Lowell.

"Hey," she said.

Lowell was obviously very anxious. "Hey. So, how do you feel?"

"Fine. How do you feel?"

"Fine. Are you still pregnant?"

Mattie Lee put her hands on her hips and sighed. "Lowell, your immaturity and lack of understanding about how a woman gets pregnant, is sometimes too much for me to bear."

"What?"

"You have the whole baby thing wrong."

"I do?"

"Yes. I am not pregnant."

"That's a relief."

Mattie Lee put her hand on his shoulder and turned him away from the house. "My Grandma Battles explained it all to me. You see, first you have to really, really, really, really love a person."

"But don't you really, really, really, really love your family?"

"Yes."

"Then you should be pregnant."

"Wait, I'm not finished. The reason I'm not pregnant is because my friend isn't visiting."

"Which friend?"

They both sat down on the stone wall. "Well, it's got to be a friend that visits every month."

"Every month?"

"Yes." Mattie Lee thinks real hard. "It's your minstrel cycle."

Lowell thought hard. "My brother has a unicycle."

She shook her head. "A minstrel cycle that visits every month and makes the girl bleed."

"Ah gawd! Cause you get into a fight and scratch each other?"

"No, the girl just bleeds."

"Ah gawd!"

"It's called a period."

Lowell looked down at the ground. "It's called disgusting."

"And it's not germs that get a girl pregnant. It's sperms."

He looked up at her completely confused. "Where do you get that?"

"You have it?"

He touched his body. "I do?"

"Yes, in your thing."

"What thing?"

"Down there," Mattie Lee said pointing to his crotch.

"In my jeans?"

"No!"

Lowell looked down at his shoe.

"No! Your dink, you dope. They're tadpoles swimming with tails."

Horrified, Lowell grabbed himself. "I have frogs in my dink?"

"So, if half-way between visits of my minstrel cycles, you stick your thing in me and then…"

"Stick it in you where?" he shouted cutting her off.

Mattie Lee gently placed her hands in her lap. "She said you have to stick it in my muffin."

"Ah, gawd!" He looked away from her knowing he was going to throw up. "And how do the frogs come out?"

"They squirm out. That's why they're called…" Having already forgotten the word, Mattie Lee struggled to find it, again. "That's why they're called…squirms, dummy! So, when they squirm into the girl, she'll get pregnant."

He got up off the stone wall and stared at her in disbelief. "Your Grandma's crazy!"

Mattie Lee stood up to defend her. "No she's not!"

"My daddy says you're all crazy and he's right! I'm going to be sick. Dinks with frogs squirming into muffins. Mamma!" screamed Lowell, as he ran back to his house crying while holding his stomach and his crotch.

"Ugh, Men," Mattie Lee declared as she ran onto the screen porch. She entered the kitchen and heard someone playing the piano in the front salon.

She skipped down to the front hallway as Trudy Lee was taking her apron off in the dining room. "I love your hair, Trudy Lee. It looks so natural like."

"I'm not sure how natural it is, but thank you Mattie Lee."

Trudy Lee put her arm around her and together they walked down towards the front salon.

"Is it Uncle Lex?"

"Yes dear," she whispered. "Go sit in front of the fire."

He was in the middle of playing *Clair de Lune.* Roscoe, who was stoking the fire, had slid his father down in the rocking chair and positioned it right next to the divan. Bert seemed surprisingly alert while Anastasia, who was sitting in the wing chair, was listening to Lex play with her eyes closed.

Lex wasn't particularly good, but what he lacked in technique he made up for in emotion. Trudy Lee walked into the salon and gently sat down on the end of the divan, closest to Bert. And as Lex played, Mona Lee descended the front staircase. She stood by the entrance of the room and listened, too.

One quarter of the way through the piece, he got to Trudy Lee's favorite part. It's a crescendo that to her always felt like a reverse waterfall. And he did play it beautifully.

No one noticed, but near the end of the piece, Bert struggled with all his strength to lift his gaunt and withered hand and placed it gently into Trudy Lee's palm. Overwhelmed with emotion, she held it as tears rolled down her cheeks.

Lex finished *Clair de Lune* and bowed his head. The room was silent.

TWELVE

SAY CHAMPAGNE

Early that same evening, Trudy Lee put thirty-six candles on one of two more pecan pies in the kitchen while she plaintively sang the last lines of *If Love Were All.*

"*But I believe, that since my life began, the most I've had is just, a talent to amuse…*"

At that moment, Mona Lee came down the back staircase.

"*Heigh-ho, if love were all.*"

"Well, I used to like that…" Mona Lee stopped mid-sentence.

Startled, Trudy Lee turned around. "What was that Mona Lee?"

"Nothing." Mona Lee didn't smile or encourage her mother to continue singing but it was her best attempt at trying to make a non-combative connection with her. "Why did you make two pies?"

"One for us and one for Lex to take back to New York City." She ran to the stairs. "Roscoe?" She shouted. "Come get your father."

Mona Lee went to the front salon as Roscoe ran down the back staircase, jumping over the fourth step and into Bert's room. Anastasia came out of Bert's bathroom wearing a new cobalt blue dress with the price tags still attached and modeled it in front of an imaginary mirror in the keeping room.

"Yes, it is a new dress and I think it's stunning," she said to her little guide with golden curls. "Oh you like it, too?"

Trudy Lee stood in the doorway, not quite believing what she was seeing.

Her mother continued. "When I saw it, it spoke to me. I just knew I had to have it."

"Anastasia Battles, who in God's name are you talking to?"

Startled, she looked over in her direction. "Just a friend."

"Well, isn't that just perfect," Trudy Lee exclaimed, throwing her arms up in the air and returning to the kitchen.

"Now, what's the matter?" Anastasia asked as she followed her.

Trudy Lee whipped around and confronted her. "You talk to everybody but me."

"Well, every time we do talk, we get into a fight."

Exasperated, she went to the cupboards and started taking down dessert plates. "Oh, never mind."

"Go ahead, Trudy Lee."

She stopped and looked up. "Do you remember if I added the fabric softener to the wash?"

"That's what you want to talk about?" Anastasia was feeling around for the pie and was just about to touch it when Trudy Lee slapped her hand away.

"No, I asked Bert if he wants a funeral and he said no."

"Well, if that's his wish?" she said flatly.

Trudy Lee started to get emotional. "But a service, even a memorial would make his life feel complete."

"To us it would."

She looked at her mother, searching for advice. "When Daddy died, you did everything the right way."

"There's no right or wrong way."

Trudy Lee grabbed the plates and took them into the dining room, as Anastasia stood in the doorway. "But Mother, his funeral was so beautiful. All of his old friends and his side of the family gathering to honor him and his life. It felt so right."

"There's something I have to confess, dear. When your father died up in Detroit I had to get him to Winston-Salem."

Trudy Lee set a plate at each setting. "Yes, you flew him down."

"No. I mailed him."

Trudy Lee stopped with a plate in mid-air, and without looking at Anastasia, she asked tentatively, "Through the post office?"

"It was cheaper. The trick was that I couldn't tell them what was in the box because it's illegal to mail bodies."

Trudy Lee turned to her as she made her way closer. "What did you say he was?"

"A grandfather's clock."

"Mother!" she exclaimed in a hushed whisper.

Anastasia touched Trudy Lee's arm. "But that's not the problem."

"Yes?"

"I mailed him to the wrong address."

Trudy Lee pulled away. "Anastasia Battles."

She brought her voice way down. "It's true. I didn't include a return address for fear that someone might find out what was inside. That's why we had a closed casket."

Trudy Lee hung her head and shook it. "My Lord."

"But we had one hell of a funeral and no one knew the better."

Her daughter looked up seriously. "Imagine the look on the person's face who opened up the box and found Papa Battles inside."

There was a moment and then they both burst into laughter.

Anastasia continued. "Eventually, I found his body and had him buried. The point is, whether you do or you don't have a service, you know how you feel in your heart."

Trudy Lee rushed back to the kitchen, grabbed a handful of forks and napkins and continued setting the table. "Yes, I do. And I also know I'm broke. I'm going to have to get a job. But I can't do anything."

Anastasia thought hard. "You could go back to being a secretary."

"Who's going to hire a..." she cleared her throat, "a sixty-four year old grandmother? Oh, I never thought my life would turn out like this."

"Now stop. It's not over yet." Trudy Lee didn't even notice that as she put forks on the right side of each plate, Anastasia, following her, moved them to the left. "Besides, you've had some beautiful experiences and a husband who has always loved you."

"Too bad he couldn't show it."

"He has in his own unique way. Bert has surrounded you with so much. Look at your four children."

Trudy Lee turned around and stared at Anastasia. "Yeah, look at them."

She couldn't help but laugh. "You know what I mean."

"And here I thought that after Bert passes I'd be on my own for the first time in my life and I could travel and then Roscoe moves back and...oh shit." Trudy Lee rushed back to the kitchen as Anastasia followed her.

"What?" she asked.

"I totally forgot," she said as she took teacups down from the cupboard. "Mona Lee thinks she killed a client out in Los Angeles and wants to move back home too."

Anastasia struggled with what she was about to say. "You know...I'm all alone too and I was thinking that... maybe...you and I...we could..."

"Live together?"

Anastasia was truly insulted. "Well, you don't have to say it like that."

"Why in God's name would you want to live with me?"

Anastasia hesitated and then started to weep. "Because I've set my apartment on fire three times and I'm being evicted."

"Mother, why didn't you tell me sooner?" Trudy Lee tried to embrace her.

"Let's not get all mushy about it," she said pushing her away. "It's about time we started…supporting each other."

Trudy Lee looked at her suspiciously. "You mean financially?"

"No, emotionally."

"I didn't know you cared that much about me."

"Well, I am your mother."

"Sometimes I wonder."

Anastasia started in on her spiel. "I carried you in my womb for nine and a half months and…"

Trudy Lee picked up on it like clockwork. "I tore your insides out because I was a breech and ruined your chances of ever having any more children."

"Well, it's the truth."

"And I'm sorry, Mother. I'm sorry I ruined your life."

Anastasia took a deep breath. "OK, OK. Let's just stop."

There was silence as Trudy Lee fidgeted with the pecan pies.

"You didn't ruin my life," Anastasia continued.

"I didn't?"

"Of course not."

There was an awkward moment of tenderness as Anastasia brushed Trudy Lee's hair away from her face.

"Well, Mother, you never say anything nice to me. You never compliment me. Say one thing you like about me. Just one."

Anastasia desperately searched for a compliment. "Ah?"

"Well?"

"You…you…"

"Yes?"

She found it. "You make the best pecan pies in the whole wide world."

Trudy Lee looked down at them. "You like my pies?"

Anastasia stuck a finger in each pecan pie and then licked it.

"Trudy Lee Martindale, I love all your damn pies. And I want the recipes."

Soaking up the compliment like a thirsty sponge, Trudy Lee embraced her. "Oh, thank you, Mother."

Roscoe dragged the rocker out of the bedroom, with Bert in it, and down to the front salon.

"We're here! We're here!" hollered Clairese from the screen porch, as Mattie Lee dashed in.

"Look at what we have! Balloons for Lex's gift opening!" shouted Mattie Lee.

Clairese opened the screen porch door for Junior, who tried to enter with thirty-six helium filled balloons. He promptly got caught in the kitchen door.

"Now, watch it Junior," warned Clairese. "Watch the door. Pull the balloons down. You're going to pop them. Wait, you better move a little to your left."

He moved to his right.

"No, your other left," Clairese cried.

Junior squeezed through the door as Clairese carried on. "Aren't they just perfect? They're so festive. It will be a festival of gifts. It was all my idea. Junior was against it, but then I talked him into it. Didn't I have a great idea?"

"Take them down to the front salon," Trudy Lee said, as she went into the dining room with the pecan pie that had the candles on it.

"OK," Clairese said, acting as the traffic cop. "Come on, Junior."

The balloons almost hit the overhead fan.

"Now, watch it," screamed Clairese. "Watch that fan. Didn't you hear me? You're not listening to me. You're going to pop one. I just know you're going to pop one."

Fed up, Junior took a pen out of his breast pocket and stabbed a balloon and it exploded.

"Fuck!" flew out of Clairese's mouth.

No one could believe what she had said as her hands flew to her mouth.

Finally, Mattie Lee broke the stunned silence. "Mamma!"

Clairese ran up the back staircase, clumping right onto the fourth step, and her foot smashed through it. "Shit!" Her hands flew to her mouth again. Horrified, she pulled her foot free and then ran up the rest of the stairs.

Junior shouted up to her. "Now, we're all full of the devil!"

Trudy Lee smiled as everyone headed for the front parlor. "I think we can fix that fourth step now."

Lex, carrying his suitcase, appeared at the top of the front staircase.

"Oh here he comes," squealed Trudy Lee. "Here comes the birthday boy."

"Mother, stop," he said.

She pulled him into the dining room as Mattie Lee went over to Grandma Battles and whispered, "You've still got the price tags on."

"I know. It's OK, darling. I'm returning it right after the party."

"Look, Lex," Trudy Lee said hugging him, "I made you another pecan pie."

"Mother, I feel so guilty about leaving."

"Nonsense. Bert wouldn't want you to miss this opportunity."

"But what if he...when I'm gone..."

"Then you'll come back." She hugged him again, more tightly. "What time is your flight?"

He looked at his watch. "I'm on standby for the 8:20."

"Oh Lex, it feels like you just got here."

"I did. I've only been here twenty-eight hours."

"That's record time," laughed Trudy Lee.

Lex walked into the front salon as Trudy Lee lit the candles on the pie and Clairese quietly crept down the stairs and into the room.

"Time to party!" yelled Trudy Lee as she turned the lights out and came into the salon carrying the pie with the candles burning. "OK everybody. Let's sing *Happy Birthday*, again."

Lex turned his back to them for a second as they began to sing.

"Happy Birthday to you..."

He turned back, wearing a pair of sunglasses, and everyone laughed.

"Happy Birthday to you, Happy Birthday dear Lex, Happy Birthday to you!"

"Make a wish," ordered Mattie Lee. "Make another wish."

Lex touched Bert's shoulder, smiled at Trudy Lee and blew out the candles. She looked at her husband and knew exactly what Lex had wished for.

"Lex, come sit on the birthday divan," Trudy Lee said as she started taking the candles off of the pie. "OK, who's first?"

"I am," Mona Lee said as she handed Lex a gift. "Use it in good health."

He unwrapped it. "Thanks Mona Lee." He held up a small porcelain object so everyone could see. "Gee, an Aladdin's lamp, I think."

"No," his sister corrected him. "It's a neti pot."

They were all at a loss.

"A nasal douche. See, you fill it with water and you shove it up one nostril and let the water flow out the other. You blow your nose and then shove it up..."

"We get the picture, Mona Lee," Trudy Lee said as she slid the pie into a box.

"Thanks," Lex said. "I bet it's great for your sinuses."

Anastasia laughed. "You should give one to Clairese."

"I don't have sinus trouble. I've told you all before, it's a deviated septum." She handed Lex a gift. "Happy Birthday."

"It's from both of us," added Junior.

Lex opened it and smiled. *"The Writer's Phrase Book.* This is great. Thanks, Clairese and Junior."

Trudy Lee handed him a card. "Here's just a little something from Dad, Grandma Battles and me."

"That's sweet," Lex said opening it up and looking at the cover. A check fell out onto the floor and he picked it up. "Oh Mother, this is too much money. I can't accept it. No, take it back."

"Lex, please," insisted Trudy Lee.

"Mother I won't cash it."

Mona Lee jumped in. "I will."

They all looked at her.

"Just kidding," she said catching herself.

"Gosh, Bro," Roscoe said, "With everything happening, I…"

Trudy Lee handed Roscoe a gift. "Dear, here's your gift to Lex."

Embarrassed, he took the gift from Trudy Lee and handed it to Lex. "Happy Birthday."

Lex opened it. "A journal. For all my secrets."

"And Mattie Lee?" encouraged Trudy Lee.

She handed Lex a card. "I made it myself, Uncle Lex."

"Thanks, sweetie," he said as he opened it up. "Oh it's beautiful." He smiled and looked up at her. "Hey, would you give me the best present of all?"

"What's that Uncle Lex?"

"Would you play your recital piece for me?"

"Sure!" She ran to the piano and sat down. She took a moment and then started Chopin's *Prelude No. 26* and she was brilliant. And when she got to the hard part where she stumbled in her recital, she paused, looked at Trudy Lee, smiled and played like crazy. And when she finished, they all, except for Bert, jumped to their feet, applauding.

Lex gave her a huge hug and then looked at his watch. "I

called Vladimir. He should be at the bottom of the drive soon."

Trudy Lee slid her arm through his. "But I thought we would all take you to the airport."

"No. I'll get too upset."

Everyone looked at each other awkwardly.

"Bert, can you hear me?" Trudy Lee touched his shoulder and he opened his eyes. "Bert, Lex has a chance to sell his children's book again. It means he'll have to leave now. What do you think?"

Slowly, he nodded yes.

"Are you sure?" Lex asked kneeling next to his chair.

Bert tried to smile.

"I'll be back as soon as I can." He kissed him on the forehead. "Thank you, Dad. Thank you for everything."

Lex went over to Clairese and embraced her.

"Bye, Lex."

He whispered to her, "If Junior says anything, listen real hard."

"Huh?"

He turned and embraced Junior. "I noticed there's a sale on Naugahyde chairs, down at the mall. I bet Clairese would look great in one."

"Thanks for letting me bend your ear."

"Hey, Rosc." He and Lex hugged. "You take care of yourself, now."

"You too."

"Please be careful," Lex added.

Mona Lee gave him an awkward hug. "Goodbye, Mona Lee."

"Maybe you should think about getting a piano, Lex."

"Thanks," he whispered as he looked over at Mattie Lee.

"Come give Uncle Tappy Toes a big hug." She jumped into his arms. "Soon you must come up to New York all by yourself and we'll go everywhere and do everything."

"Great," she said as he put her down. "Hey, Grandma." He fell into her embrace.

"You OK, Lex?"

He started to tremble. "No."

"Then keep an eye out for you know who."

Lex looked at Trudy Lee, who had tears welling up in her eyes. "Well, for crying out loud. Look at us. You'd think Lex was never coming back."

They all forced a laugh.

"Dear, hurry," Trudy Lee said as she held Lex tightly. "Go back to New York and give them your best shot. Oh, here. Don't forget your birthday pie. And I've put all your gifts in this bag." She handed them to him. "We all love you."

"Me too, you," he said as he reached for his luggage in the front hall.

"Wait!" Trudy Lee ran into the dining room.

They all looked at each other and shook their heads as she darted away, knowing exactly what she was up to. But as exhausting and, at times, infuriating as Trudy Lee was, they acquiesced to her eccentric and unpredictable whims, for all knew she was loving them the only way she knew how. And in truth, she was the egg that was holding the Martindale recipe together.

As they heard her cursing while rifling through a closet, they all turned to Bert who had enough strength to give them a shrug of his shoulders, which clearly meant, *Why the hell not?*

"I know you all hate this," she said running back. "But it will only take a second."

She reappeared with her camera attached to a tripod and smiled from ear to ear. The entire family was ready for the shot. She set the timer and ran to join them.

"One, two, three," counted Trudy Lee, and they all shouted, "Champagne!"

THIRTEEN

TEAROOM FOR TWO

"I didn't make it onto the 8:20 flight," Lex shouted into the phone as his voice cracked. "Vladimir stood me up. I trudged back up the drive and Junior brought me to the airport." A woman carrying a wailing baby slowly walked by Lex as he sneezed.

"You OK?" asked Peter.

Lex blew his nose. "What? I can't hear you."

"I asked, are you OK?"

"I feel like…"

Just then, an annoying beeping sound started up as a passenger cart carrying three obese women emerged. The driver, oblivious to all pedestrians, backed up dangerously close to Lex doing a three-point turn, and managed to run over the tip of his left shoe.

"Noooo! Oh, nooooo!" cried Lex. He was more concerned about his Prada than his pride as he kicked off his shoe and examined it.

"What?" shouted Peter. "What's going on?"

"Watch where you're going," cried Lex as he slipped it back on. "I was about to say that I feel like I've been run over by a

Mack truck…and now I have." He coughed. "And I'm losing my voice."

"When's the next plane?"

"11:45. It's the last flight."

"Are you going to call home and have someone come get you?"

An extremely loud announcement came over the PA system. "No," laughed Lex. "I think I'd rather wait it out here. It's quieter and calmer."

There was a long pause. Lex knew what Peter was going to ask next and actually mouthed the words with him.

"Did you tell Trudy Lee?"

Again, he laughed. He was going to say no, but then changed his mind.

"Yes. I did tell her."

"And how did she take it?"

"The only way my mother could."

"That's good. You got that out of the way."

"Yeah."

"Should I wait up?" Peter asked genuinely concerned.

"No. Don't bother."

"Try to get some sleep."

"Yeah right."

He hung up the phone and thought about the lie he had just told Peter, and then realized Trudy Lee did know something was wrong. She may have been a drama queen but she wasn't stupid. She read between the lines. In fact, he felt confident that everyone in his family had enough pieces of the puzzle to know that something was terribly wrong. They had taken a vow not to speak of it, couldn't speak of it, or in Trudy Lee's case, wouldn't speak of it. And for right now, that was OK.

Lex surveyed the waiting area. Feeling totally constipated, he went off to use the men's room. And while sitting in that same stall next to the same urinal, he saw the same pair of scuffed beige Timberland boots reappear. And again, there were no signs of pee. But from the shadows, there was every indication that the phantom stroker was striking again.

Another man entered and stood at the urinal next to him. This all intrigued Lex to no end, however he was just too tired to play. And as he sat there with his head resting against the stall, watching the shadow stroking harder and harder, the door to the men's room suddenly burst open. In a flash, the local SWAT team of the Raleigh/Durham North Carolina Airport Authority stormed the men's room.

"Let go of your member and put your hands behind your back!" they ordered.

Instinctively, Lex pulled his feet up so they wouldn't notice him in the stall.

"You're under arrest!"

The cops quickly handcuffed the perpetrator and read him his Miranda Rights. It turned out that the man was being watched by the police after they had received a tip that he was guilty of lewd public conduct at the terminal.

"I want to call my fucking lawyer!" screamed the offender.

Lex perked up. He knew that voice. As they were hauling him out, he peeped through the stall door crack and saw that it was Delbert Lovejoy.

"Jesus fucking Christ," he whispered as he smiled and looked up to the heavens. "There is a God, after all."

ABOUT THE AUTHOR

Arthur Wooten is the author of the critically acclaimed books *Dizzy, Leftovers, On Picking Fruit* and *Fruit Cocktail.* He's also penned the children's picture book *Wise Bear William: A New Beginning* and the collection of short stories, *Arthur Wooten's Shorts.* A playwright, his works include the award winning *Birthday Pie,* which had its world premiere at the Waterfront Playhouse, Key West, FL. His one act plays, *Lily* and *The Lunch,* have been produced in New York and most recently in Te Anau, New Zealand. For two years he was the humorist for the London based magazine, reFRESH. Arthur grew up in Andover, MA, and now resides in New York City.

www.arthurwooten.com